NO MORE WAITING

As soon as Skye and the woman were alone in the room, she flung off her gown and stood proudly before him.

He looked her over. She was a column of dusky flesh, with long thighs tapering up from her trim calves. Her hips arced dramatically into the curve of her narrow waist, and above them her beautiful full bosom swelled challengingly.

"I've been looking a long time for you, Donna," Skye said, thinking of the men he had killed, and who had tried to kill him, as he followed her trail.

She smiled. "Was it worth the wait, Skye?"

That was exactly what the Trailsman was aiming to find out—right now. . . .

Exciting Westerns by Jon Sharpe from SIGNET

(0451)

☐ THE TRAILSMAN #1: SEVEN WAGONS WEST (127293—$2.50)*
☐ THE TRAILSMAN #2: THE HANGING TRAIL (132939—$2.50)*
☐ THE TRAILSMAN #3: MOUNTAIN MAN KILL (121007—$2.50)
☐ THE TRAILSMAN #4: THE SUNDOWN SEARCHERS (122003—$2.50)
☐ THE TRAILSMAN #5: THE RIVER RAIDERS (111990—$2.25)
☐ THE TRAILSMAN #6: DAKOTA WILD (119886—$2.50)
☐ THE TRAILSMAN #7: WOLF COUNTRY (123697—$2.50)
☐ THE TRAILSMAN #8: SIX-GUN DRIVE (121724—$2.50)
☐ THE TRAILSMAN #9: DEAD MAN'S SADDLE (126629—$2.50)*
☐ THE TRAILSMAN #10: SLAVE HUNTER (114655—$2.25)
☐ THE TRAILSMAN #11: MONTANA MAIDEN (116321—$2.25)
☐ THE TRAILSMAN #12: CONDOR PASS (118375—$2.50)*
☐ THE TRAILSMAN #13: BLOOD CHASE (119274—$2.50)*
☐ THE TRAILSMAN #14: ARROWHEAD TERRITORY (120809—$2.50)*
☐ THE TRAILSMAN #15: THE STALKING HORSE (121430—$2.50)*
☐ THE TRAILSMAN #16: SAVAGE SHOWDOWN (122496—$2.50)*
☐ THE TRAILSMAN #17: RIDE THE WILD SHADOW (122801—$2.50)*

*Prices slightly higher in Canada

THE TRAILSMAN 50

BLOOD OATH

by

Jon Sharpe

A SIGNET BOOK

NEW AMERICAN LIBRARY

PUBLISHER'S NOTE

This novel is a work of fiction. Names, characters, places, and incidents either are the product of the author's imagination or are used fictitiously, and any resemblance to actual persons, living or dead, events, or locales is entirely coincidental.

Copyright © 1986 by Jon Sharpe

The first chapter of this book previously appeared in *The Swamp Slayers*, the forty-ninth book in this series.

SIGNET TRADEMARK REG. U.S. PAT. OFF. AND FOREIGN COUNTRIES
REGISTERED TRADEMARK—MARCA REGISTRADA
HECHO EN CHICAGO, U.S.A.

SIGNET, SIGNET CLASSIC, MENTOR, PLUME, MERIDIAN and NAL BOOKS
are published by New American Library,
1633 Broadway, New York, New York 10019

First Printing, February, 1986

1 2 3 4 5 6 7 8 9

The Trailsman

Beginnings . . . they bend the tree and they mark the man. Skye Fargo was born when he was eighteen. Terror was his midwife, vengeance his first cry. Killing spawned Skye Fargo, ruthless, cold-blooded murder. Out of the acrid smoke of gunpowder still hanging in the air, he rose, cried out a promise never forgotten.

The Trailsman, they began to call him, all across the West: searcher, scout, hunter, the man who could see where others only looked, his skills for hire but not his soul, the man who lived each day to the fullest, yet trailed each tomorrow. Skye Fargo, the Trailsman, the seeker who could take the wildness of a land and the wanting of a woman and make them his own.

*1861—New Mexico Territory,
where gold fever ignites the passions
of men and women . . .*

1

The Trailsman swore and flung another shot at the rocks above him. An answering fusillade caused him to duck down and simmer in frustration while the rounds, like angry hornets, ricocheted about his head and shoulders.

"Shit," he muttered furiously as he swiftly reloaded his Colt.

Known as the Trailsman in countless towns and settlements throughout the West, his name was Skye Fargo. A large, powerful man all of six feet tall, with enormous shoulders and an upper torso alive with muscles that stood out like mole tunnels, the Trailsman had a thick mop of unruly jet-black hair, lake-blue eyes, and an alert, hawklike face with a nose seemingly fashioned out of granite and with a jaw to match. Dressed in deerskin shirt and pants, he wore a heavy gun belt about his narrow waist, from which depended his Colt's holster.

Having finished reloading his Colt, he peered through his hawklike eyes at the rocks high above him on the canyon rim and shook his head in frustration. From the very beginning, this foray south of the border had brought him nothing but trouble. And now it looked as if the herd of prime horseflesh he and this scabrous outfit were driving to Tularosa just might not make it after all. Served him right for trying to do two things at once—make himself rich while chasing after those two gunslicks he had heard about. As it turned out, they hadn't been the men he was searching for, and a less-determined man would have been discouraged.

Among the rocks above, an Apache showed his head. Fargo waited. After the Apache's head came his shoulders. A bleak smile on his face, Fargo fired. The Apache went reeling back out of sight, giving Fargo some comfort.

First had come the *bandidos* and now these children from hell. They must have traded for Spencer repeaters, and they were now firing down at them with more enthusiasm than skill. Otherwise, not one of Fargo's men would have escaped this ambush. But the Apaches' fire had been enough to down two of his men. One was dead, another badly wounded.

Turning about, Fargo peered down the canyon and was relieved to see the rest of his outfit driving the herd out of the canyon, heading north for Tularosa. The dust kicked up by the herd almost obscured them, but it looked as if most of the horses had eluded the Apaches. That was something, at least. Soon, Fargo expected, some of his men would peel back to give him a hand with these damn Apaches. The herd kept moving, and before long the dust had settled back to earth behind them, revealing an empty trail.

Fargo turned back to the Apaches. They occupied the high rocks on the southern rim of the canyon, and their inaccurate fusillade was constant enough to be dangerous. Dirty and dog-tired, the Trailsman lifted his head warily to let his eyes search the rim-rocks above. Seeing nothing, he turned, and keeping his tall frame hunched so that it wouldn't be skylined, he moved swiftly down the steep slope to the nearest of his two downed men.

His name was Tom Rifkin. Fargo grabbed his shoulder and rolled him over. The bullet had caught Rifkin in the neck and ranged up into his skull. The skin under his right eye was puffy and black. Over Rifkin's bloody mouth swarmed a cluster of green-bellied flies. Fargo nudged Rifkin back over onto his belly and glanced skyward. The buzzards were already coasting in the hot updrafts high above the canyon floor, like giant cinders from a wood fire. Leaving Rifkin, Fargo continued down the slope to his other wounded partner, Walt Tennyson.

Of all the men he had recruited for this drive, Fargo respected and liked Walt Tennyson the most. Walt, propped up against a boulder, grinned at Fargo through pain-slitted eyes. As Fargo knelt beside him, Walt started to say something, but instead began to cough weakly, wiping sweat off his pale forehead with the back of his forearm. His hat had tumbled off his head and lay on its crown some distance down the slope. The neat bullet hole in Walt's sweat-darkened checked shirt was just above the fleshy part of his left shoulder.

"How you doing, Walt?" Fargo asked.

"I'll live," he told Fargo. "Where's the horses?"

Fargo gestured with his head. "Down the slope."

The man turned his head to see for himself. Walt's sorrel was standing in the shade of a boulder, its still-heaving sides dripping with sweat. Beside it, idly cropping the grass under the boulder, was Fargo's pinto. Fargo wondered if the Apaches' persistence might possibly be related to an eagerness on their part to gain possession of his mount. The Ovaro was a handsome, powerful animal—qualities the Apaches would sure as hell appreciate.

"I can make it that far by myself," Walt said. "Give me a hand, will you?"

Fargo helped the man to his feet, and with Walt's right arm slung around Fargo's shoulder, the two men started down the treacherous, shale-littered slope. They were almost to Walt's horse when a round from almost directly overhead slammed into Walt. He went sprawling facedown. Fargo whirled, caught sight of the Apache outlined against the bright, cloudless sky, and sent two quick shots up at him. The Apache dropped his rifle and toppled from his perch.

Keeping low, Fargo crabbed sideways to examine

Walt. The man gasped in panic, "Jesus, Fargo, this time I'm hurt bad!"

Examining him closely, Fargo saw that the second slug had entered high on Walt's shoulder.

"Where does it hurt?" he asked.

"That's just it! I got no feelin' in my legs," Walt told him, his eyes bugging wide with astonishment. "I can't move them! My God, Fargo, I'm paralyzed."

A sudden flurry of more rifle fire sent rounds whining among the rocks all around them. Keeping his head down, Fargo studied the entrance wound and saw where the round must have ranged down his back and across the spine, severing it.

Fargo started to drag the big man down the slope toward the horses. His intention was to tie Walt over his saddle, then lead Walt's sorrel out of the canyon. Just before he reached the sorrel, however, an unseen marksman above him fired three spaced shots, the slugs kicking up dust a dozen yards short of Fargo. A fourth bullet whined past Fargo's head and caromed off a ledge behind him, slamming into Walt's sorrel and catching the animal in the chest. Its forelegs buckled as if they had been cut off at the knees. Threshing its legs feebly as it lay on his side, the sorrel let out one last shrill cry and died.

"Fargo, I ain't goin' to make it," Walt gasped weakly.

"Sure, you are," Fargo insisted as he looked back up at the rocks for the Apaches. The bastards had ducked back down, but he caught their shadows and saw how close they were getting as they kept inching closer.

Fargo glanced down the canyon. Shit! When were those damn men of his going to double back to give him a hand?

"Fargo," Walt said, "I got something important to tell you. I want you to listen."

"I'm listening," the Trailsman said, still squinting up at the rocks through the blazing sun. "Go ahead."

"I want to give my share of this herd to Donna Alvarez in Tularosa."

Fargo glanced in surprise down at Walt. "Donna Alvarez? Who the hell is she?"

"Never mind that. She's the one bankrolled me, gave me the stake to join this damned enterprise. I want her to have my share. Will you see to it?"

Fargo was amazed at the request. Not once during this entire operation had Walt mentioned this woman's name. "You sure about this, Walt?"

"Just give me your word. I want her to have my share!"

"Hell, it's too early to count yourself out, Walt."

"Don't give me no bullshit. You know I'm a dead man. Now give me your word."

Fargo hesitated only a moment, then shrugged. "Okay, Walt. You got my word."

"Now kill me."

Fargo pulled back. "You gone loco?"

"No. My head is clear. It's my body from the waist down that's gone. But that still leaves the

Apache with plenty to play with. So you got to kill me, Fargo."

"That's crazy talk," Fargo told him. "Soon as Clint or Slats gets back here to give us a hand, we'll get you out of here. Just keep your ass low."

Walt laughed then, a bitter, miserable croak. "Hell, Fargo! They ain't comin' back for us. They figure we bought it by now. That means bigger shares for them." Walt dropped his head and began to cough dryly.

Fargo knew at once the man was telling the truth. He glanced back up at the rimrocks. The Apaches were still advancing, using boulders and protruding ledges for cover; they were like shadows inching along the canyon, gray ghosts with pale headbands prowling in the afternoon. Fargo knew he'd taught them some respect for his shoothing, anyway. There were only five, maybe six, Apaches left.

Fargo uncorked his canteen and held it to Walt's lips. Walt gulped feebly at the water. Then Fargo took a swallow himself, the cold neck of the canteen pulling painfully on his cracked lips.

"You better get out of here, Fargo," Walt gasped, "while you still can."

Fargo nodded. He was thinking the same thing. But he couldn't leave without Walt—or, at least, without first making another effort to get him out.

Abruptly, two successive slugs struck the ground so close that dirt and shards of rock kicked up into Fargo's face, momentarily blinding him. Fargo flung up his gun hand to protect his eyes, then scanned the rimrock. He spotted the figures moving swiftly along the rim toward the canyon mouth. If he didn't move out of there fast, they'd soon have him cut off.

Holstering his Colt, Fargo grabbed Walt under the armpits and began to drag his deadweight across the open ground toward the Ovaro. With Walt draped over the pinto's neck, Fargo could mount up and make a run for it. But a sudden, concentrated flurry of rifle fire poured down on them, forcing Fargo to leave Walt and take shelter behind a boulder.

The Apaches were too close now—and Fargo would never make it out of the canyon with Walt. He glanced down at the Ovaro. The pony was standing back in among some rocks, tossing his head and occasionally pawing the ground before going back to the grass he was cropping. He was a courageous, powerful animal, but there was no way he could carry both men any great distance—not with a passel of Apaches on their tail.

Fargo looked back at Walt. He was lying face-down in the dust, his fingers digging into the ground.

"Walt!"

The man raised his head.

"Can you crawl over here?"

Walt began to drag his paralyzed body toward Fargo. His progress was agonizingly slow.

As Fargo waited, a slug sang off the boulder inches above his head. Wincing, Fargo ducked lower. "Come on, Walt," he urged.

Walt glanced up. "I told you, Fargo. I'm paralyzed. Leave me."

"Shit! I don't want to do that, Walt."

"You ain't got no choice. You stay any longer, they'll get you, too!"

Fargo squinted up at the rocks. Walt spoke the truth. He glimpsed one Apache not a hundred yards above him. Before the Indian ducked out of sight, Fargo saw the Indian's face clearly, his anthracite eyes shining in his broad pan of a face. Before Fargo could lift his Colt, the face vanished.

"Kill me, Fargo," Walt pleaded. "Don't leave me to these devils."

Fargo felt cold sweat standing out on his forehead. He knew he would be doing Walt a favor, but that didn't make it any easier. Painfully, unhappily, he drew his Colt and aimed at the man staring up at him.

"Don't forget your promise, Fargo."

"I won't. Now turn your head, dammit!"

Obediently, Walt turned his head and closed his eyes.

Aiming carefully at a spot just behind Walt's ears, Fargo pulled the trigger.

It took only one shot.

Afterward, riding up the canyon astride his Ovaro, Fargo comforted himself with the thought of just how much more merciful for Walt that single, annihilating bullet had been when compared to the slow, terrible death the Apaches would have visited upon him.

It was some comfort—but not much.

The Apaches, mounted up as well, were hard on his tail, their Spencers blasting, slugs whining off the rocks around him. The Apaches knew the herd was gone, but cheated of Walt, they now wanted Fargo to hang facedown over a fire.

The canyon trail became rapidly steeper, turning into a series of tilted slab rock benches that rose to a narrow pass. The afternoon's slanting sunlight left a hand of shadow along the west wall, but the heat was merciless. It sucked moisture from Fargo's shirt and crusted the soapy lather on the Ovaro's sweat-stained neck. Fargo peered up at the narrow slot of the pass and wondered if the Ovaro would be able to make it that far.

But he lasted, as Fargo knew he would. Dismounting at the first outcropping of rock that offered protection, Fargo tied the mount to a clump of manzanita, lifted his Sharps from the saddle scabbard, and dropped a linen cartridge into the breach. Slamming up the trigger guard, he settled down behind a low boulder to wait.

The Apaches halted nearly a quarter of a mile down the canyon. They had seen him dismount and knew well enough how easy it would be for Fargo to hold them off from his high vantage point. There was a long interval of waiting as the frustrated Apaches milled about, palavering. Abruptly, the decision went to Fargo as the Apaches broke and raced back down the canyon and out of sight.

Fargo climbed up onto a rock to watch the dust settle back on the trail behind them. When he was certain they were gone, he mounted back up and headed after the herd, his angry thoughts now centered on the remaining three men of his outfit who had made no effort to ride back to give a hand. The plan had been for Fargo, Walt, and Rifkin to hang back and slow the Apaches—with the others to return as soon as the herd was safe. Before leaving Fargo and the others, Clint, Slats, and Yank Mosely had promised Fargo they would do just that.

But the trail ahead of Fargo was empty of riders. Not one of those bastards had turned back. Walt had been right. The men were interested only in seeing an increase in their share of what the herd would bring.

Now that he was out of danger, Fargo allowed his exhausted pinto to plod slowly along. Soon it was night, and he didn't realize he was dozing until he almost tipped out of the saddle. Remembering a night-herd trick an old-timer had taught him, he loosened his holster belt to the last hole, then looped it around the saddle horn. It held him snubbed tight to the pommel.

The last thing he remembered before falling off to sleep was his promise to Walt Tennyson—a goddamn blood oath, he grunted—but an oath he intended to keep.

2

The pinto's eager whinny awoke Fargo. For a moment he had no idea where he was until his eyes focused and he saw the campfire just ahead and heard Yank call, "Who is it?"

Fargo realized then that the pinto had overtaken the herd. They were still in the mountains. The air was cool. Must be late evening, Fargo reckoned, and he wondered how long he had slept asaddle. As he came into the circle of firelight, Clint came over to stand by Yank.

"Where's Tom and Walt?" Yank asked. His big, shambling body cast a barrel-shape shadow before him on the ground.

"Dead," Fargo said, lifting his holster belt over the saddle horn.

As he stepped down, Clint—a round man with a

sagging belly—took a step closer and peered at him intently. "Ain't you hurt none?"

"I was lucky."

"Too bad about Walt—and Tom."

"We were expecting some help from you three soon as the herd cleared the canyon," Fargo told them.

Clint looked nervously at Yank, then back at Fargo. "We gave it some thought."

"Yeah," admitted Yank. "But that's all we gave it." There was a cold smile on his long, horsy face.

"What he means is," said Clint, "we figured it wouldn't do us any good to lose everything by going back into that canyon. We figured you three could handle it—and if you couldn't, there'd be no sense in us trying."

Clint hauled his belt back up over his sagging belly. "And we had the herd to think of," he added.

"Sure you did," said Fargo. "And the fewer there were, the bigger the shares."

Yank smiled, his large square teeth gleaming in the campfire. "That's the way of it, Fargo."

"For some, maybe. Where's Slats?"

"Watching the herd."

"You think he's enough?"

"Them horses are plumb tired out, Fargo. And it's a clear, cool night. No chance of them spooking."

Fargo nodded. "You got any coffee?"

"Sure," said Clint, turning back to the fire.

Fargo unsaddled his pinto, wiped off his back, and let him loose. The Ovaro whickered his delight

21

as he trotted down the slight slope to join the other saddle horses on the flat below the camp.

Fargo sat down on a log and took the coffee Clint handed him. It was as black as an Apache's soul and quickly smote the dull, nodding lethargy that still clouded his senses, bringing back his usual clarity of perception, which made him acutely aware of the two men's alert watchfulness as they stood around him. More than once during the drive north they had experienced his anger and were expecting him to erupt now. They had just admitted their lack of interest in going back to help him, so now they were bracing themselves for trouble, ready to slap it right back at him when it came.

Fargo said nothing, however, as he sipped the black coffee. He smiled grimly to himself at the thought of how they'd take the news that Walt's share was going to some whore in Tularosa—a dame named Donna Alvarez.

Fargo finished his coffee and glanced around at the waiting men. "How much of the herd got through?"

"We lost about ten, maybe twelve."

"That all?"

"That's all," said Clint, his voice heavy with pride—and menace.

"You think maybe we could make that Confederate officer pay a little more?" Yank asked hopefully. "I hear that war back East is really starting to heat up."

"Maybe," said Fargo.

Clint smiled. "Split four ways, that should make

us at least five hundred richer. That won't be so hard to take."

Fargo took out one of his last cheroots and snipped off one end with his bowie. Then he reached over, grabbed a blazing faggot, and lit the smoke. Leaning back, he inhaled deeply, then glanced up at the two men.

"You got that wrong. It'll be split five ways."

"What the hell are you talking about?" demanded Yank.

"Walt left his share to a woman in Tularosa."

"He did what?" Clint demanded.

"You heard me."

"Shit," said Yank. "We don't have to pay no attention to that. Who is this dame, anyway—some whore he picked up?"

"I don't know."

"What's this about a woman?"

Fargo glanced over to see Slats Tarnell's tall, lean frame walking up the slope to the campfire. He had dismounted on the flat below, leaving the herd untended. Fargo didn't like that, but he decided to say nothing about it yet.

Yank turned to Slats. "Tom and Walt are dead."

"But Walt left his share of the herd to a whore in Tularosa," Clint finished. "Donna Alvarez. You ever hear Walt tell of her?"

"Nope," Slats replied. "Probably some cat-house dolly he took a fancy to." Slats hunkered down beside the fire and reached for the coffeepot. Standing up with his filled cup, he said, "Which one of you is going to relieve me?"

"I will," Yank said. "But what's the hurry? The Apaches are behind us now."

Slats shrugged and looked appraisingly down at Fargo. "Glad to see you made it, Fargo," he said. "We knew you could handle the Apaches—or we'd have gone back to help."

Fargo got to his feet. "If you had, maybe Walt and Tom Rifkin would still be alive."

Slats moved his broad, bony shoulders in an idle shrug. "Maybe. Maybe not. Now, what's this about Walt leaving his share to a whore?"

"It ain't been established yet that she is a whore."

"It don't matter what she is. We don't have to pay no attention to what that fool Walt said. We're still going to split four ways."

Fargo shook his head. "No, we're not. This woman staked Walt. She's entitled to her share, and I promised Walt she'd get it."

"You mean we ain't got no say in it?"

"I mean I gave Walt my word. And she staked him. That's good enough for me."

"Well, it ain't good enough for me."

Fargo smiled at him. "You aiming to change my mind for me?"

Slats tossed the rest of his coffee into the fire. "It's three against one, Fargo. We already took a vote, looks like. So that means we split the profits four ways, not five."

"Who elected you boss of this outfit?"

Slats smiled coldly. "Why, Yank and Clint did. While you was back there playing with them

24

injuns. You talk big, Fargo. But I never heard of you before you organized this here expedition. You been telling us when to dance, sure enough—but maybe now it's our turn to make you hop."

Chuckling, Fargo reached down for his bedroll and saddle. Resting the saddle on one shoulder, he looked around for a place to sack out. He espied some high ground and was heading for it when Slats cleared his throat.

"Fargo?"

Fargo held up and turned around.

"You ain't calling me?"

"What for?"

"For speaking up and taking this horse herd."

Fargo chuckled. "Hell, Slats, you're not taking anything." He turned back around, trudged up onto the rise, and set down his saddle and bedroll. He was bone-tired, but not too weary to take his Colt from his holster and place it under his saddle as he flung the soogan's flap over his shoulder, lay his head down upon the saddle, and went to sleep.

It was a sullen, unhappy crew that Fargo saw hunched around the morning campfire, waiting for him to join them. Fargo made no effort to hurry. Dawn was a cold, streak of light on the far horizon, and the ground was sopping wet from the heavy dew. The meadowland far below was covered with pockets of mist. The horse herd milled peacefully, at least a thousand head of prime horseflesh they had purchased from the Mexican authorities in

Sonora for a fraction of the price they would now bring as mounts for the Confederate cavalry.

Yank had put together a breakfast of bacon and beans and coffee. Fargo ate heartily. When he finished his coffee, he turned on his waiting crew. "We'll be driving the herd to Diablo Creek outside of Tularosa," he told them. "Wait for me there while I scare up this here Confederate lieutenant."

"Hell, Fargo," Slats told him, "you can't give no orders to us. I told you last night. I'm in charge now."

Fargo turned to peer at Tarnell. The big lanky son of a bitch was looking a bit anxious, but he'd had a night to think things over and was still convinced he had the sand to take these horses and this crew away from Fargo. Come to think of it, he'd been acting like a mule with a bur up his ass for some time now.

Fargo reached down for his saddle and straightened, balancing it on his shoulder. Then he picked up his bedroll. As he stood there, his muscles flexing easily under the saddle's burden, his lake-blue eyes alert after the good night's sleep, his belly full, he smiled coldly at Slats. "If you're in charge, you fool son of a bitch—then *take* charge."

The other two backed up a few steps to give Slats the room he was going to need if he insisted on playing out his hand. Tarnell crouched slowly, his eyes boring into Fargo's, then went for his gun. Fargo heaved the saddle. It caught Slats in the chest, bowling him backward. He went down heavily on his back, the gun jarring loose from his grasp,

Fargo's saddle tumbling on past him down the slope.

Slats started to scramble back up onto his feet. Fargo stepped closer and kicked the man in the face, catching Tarnell squarely on the nose. Slats' head rocked back; blood gushed from his broken snout. He lay on his back for a moment, staring up at Fargo through tearing eyes, one hand clapped over his bubbling nose. The blood flow was so thick, Tarnell started to choke and then cough violently. Heaving uncontrollably, he pushed himself to a sitting position and tried to wipe his nose.

Thoroughly beaten, the man sat there, blood flowing down his chin, his eyes red, his slim shoulders hunched pathetically as he gagged on his own blood. Fargo kicked Tarnell's Colt away, then hunkered down beside him and peered into his smashed face.

"You still want to run this outfit, Slats?"

Tarnell hesitated, but only for an instant. Then he shook his head miserably.

"Fine. Now listen. The next time you draw on me, I'll kill you."

Slats stared back at him then, and in Tarnell's eyes, Fargo saw a hatred so implacable, he wondered if he had been wise in letting this lanky troublemaker live.

With a shrug, Fargo stood up and turned to the others. They could have struck at him while he was working Slats over, but their fear of him had held them back. Now they shifted uneasily, wondering what Fargo might do to them.

There was no friendship here, Fargo reflected, no bond of shared danger and desperate survival. Greed was the core of this partnership, and had Fargo not been so intent on tracking those two men he'd been hunting for so long, he would've noticed that when he'd convinced this motley crew to join him six months earlier. The hope for gain was all that had welded them together—and it spawned no loyalty, only a snarling, dog-eat-dog brutality.

Not one of these men had said a word about their two dead partners back there. Their share of the herd was all they were concerned about. They must have been three very unhappy men when Fargo rode into the circle of their campfire the night before. His survival had taken gold out of their pockets.

"You still going to give Walt's share to that woman?" Yank asked.

Fargo bent to pick up his bedroll. He said nothing. He was through arguing the matter. They interpreted his silence correctly, however, and took a step closer, like dogs hoping for one more chomp on the bone.

"Dammit, Fargo," Clint protested, "she's probably just some slut, one of them big-breasted whores at Ma Toady's."

"That's right," insisted Yank. "Clint's telling the truth. Do you think it's fair for one of them whores to get a share after what we done to bring this herd through the *bandidos* and Apaches?"

"We rode our asses off getting them horses out of Sonora," Clint persisted.

"Dammit, Fargo," Yank cried, "you ain't listening."

Fargo looked at them with cool contempt. "That's right. It'll be a cold day in hell before I listen to the likes of you two."

He shoved roughly on past them down the slope to pick up his saddle. He didn't look back, but he could feel the malignant stares of his three partners boring into his back. Fargo wasn't afraid they'd cut him down from behind. Not now. They were too cowardly for that, and they had seen what had happened to Slats Tarnell.

But later—maybe some dark night—one of them, Slats probably, would fill himself up with bravo juice and try again. Fargo smiled grimly.

3

Fargo arrived in Tularosa shortly before nightfall. Passing the stock pens at the town's southern end, he observed that Main Street seemed unchanged for the most part. There was the courthouse, the Apache Basin Bank, and Morgan's Mercantile, with the Tularosa Hotel, Sutter's Barbershop, and the Wells Fargo office on the opposite side. One long block west of Main Street and running parallel to it was a broad avenue, resplendent with its ancient mission and its tree-shaded homes.

There was little traffic. A saddled horse stood at the hitch rack in front of the bank, and a team was pulled up at the mercantile loading platform. Two men sat on the hotel veranda, and a shoeless Mexican boy with a wood-laden burro came out of the alley behind the livery as Fargo headed toward it. On the next corner, between the Shamrock Saloon and Huffmeyer's blacksmith shop sat Ma Toady's parlor house, the sagging front stoop and shuttered windows a familiar sight to Fargo. He'd visited Ma's place one whiskey-fogged night before setting out for Sonora.

Old Amos Ledbetter sat in his livery stable's wide doorway. Fargo dismounted and led his pinto toward the entrance. The old man got to his feet, peering at Fargo. The man hadn't bothered to shave in the past couple of days, and his gaunt cheeks were covered with white stubble.

"Don't I know you?" Ledbetter said.

"Yup. Six months ago."

"That's right. Skye Fargo." He scratched his bristly cheek. "You went south with them no-accounts, looking for horseflesh."

"That's me," Fargo said, pulling up in front of the old man.

"See you still got that pretty Ovaro. Looks a mite gaunt, though."

"He is. Take good care of him."

"That I will," Ledbetter said, stepping forward to take the pinto's rein. " 'Bout time you showed up. There's a right purty-looking Confederate officer in the hotel been looking for you."

"When did he ride in?"

"A week ago."

"Thanks, Amos."

As Ledbetter started to lead the pinto into the barn, Fargo told him he would be in for his gear later, then flipped him a coin. Ledbetter snatched it out of the air with impressive dexterity.

"One more thing," Fargo called after him.

Ledbetter halted.

"You hear tell of Donna Alvarez?"

The old man's face screwed into a frown as he tried to recall. "Nope," he said. "Less'n she's one of Ma Toady's girls—or working in that new Fancy Anne parlor farther down the street."

"No. She wouldn't be a new girl."

Ledbetter shrugged and showed his yellow teeth in a hapless grin. "I can't help you, Fargo. I don't have the resources to plow them fields no more. You're asking the wrong feller."

Fargo grinned back at Ledbetter. "Thanks anyway."

Before registering at the hotel, Fargo stopped in at Morgan's for some fresh clothing, then tramped into the barbershop for a hot bath and a shave, after which he dumped his sweat-soiled buckskins in a Chinese laundry and walked over to the hotel and registered. He checked his room out, then went back down to the hotel bar for a look-around. He didn't see the Confederate officer, but that didn't bother him any. He'd find him soon enough, and at the moment he was interested in finding a thick steak smothered in onions. He hadn't eaten since morning and was ravenous.

He was on his way across the street to the restaurant when he heard his name called. He turned and saw Lt. Maxfield Scott, a relieved smile on his face, hurrying down the hotel's veranda steps.

"Join me in supper," Fargo said, shaking the

lieutenant's hand heartily. "I'm as hungry as a June bear."

"I'd be delighted," Scott said as the two men dodged a team of dray horses and finished crossing the street.

An hour later, they had finished their meal and were lighting up when Lt. Scott inquired somewhat nervously if Fargo was sure he could trust his somewhat disaffected men to bring the horses safely to Diablo Creek.

"They want that gold you promised in payment," Fargo assured Scott. "They'll be there."

Scott sighed. "Then there's no way I can convince you to accept Confederate currency? I assure you, Fargo, the bills are most fresh and crisp, printed less than a month ago in Richmond."

"It was gold we settled on."

"Yes, of course." The lieutenant sighed. "Forgive me. I was just following orders. My superiors had instructed me to do what I could to convince you of the worth of our new currency in the hope that you might consent to accept it in lieu of gold. I won't bring the matter up again. My conscience is clear."

"You have the gold?"

"Gold dust. From our agents in California. It is resting safely in the bank. Tomorrow I'll withdraw it and bring it with me when my men and I ride out to take over the herd. When do you expect the horses to arrive at Diablo Creek?"

"Early afternoon at the latest."

"Excellent. I don't have to remind you, I'm sure,

of the urgency of this mission. The North has all the resources, it seems—the South only a multitude of gallant men willing to die for the independence of their homeland. I hope it'll be enough."

"You have my sympathy, Lieutenant. This here War Between the States doesn't make any kind of sense to me, so I'm not about to take sides. I have my own war to fight out here."

Scott frowned in sympathy. "I presume you mean those two men you were after. Tell me, did you find either of them?"

"I found one of the men I was trailing."

"Was he one of those who—"

"No."

"I'm sorry. This means your search goes on."

"Yes."

Lt. Scott finished his coffee and stood up. "Well, then. I must take leave now so that I can get my men ready. I wish you'd think over my request to return to Mexico for more horses."

"I'll think it over, but that's all I can promise, Lieutenant."

With a casual salute, the lieutenant left. Fargo watched him go—a very young man in a handsome new uniform, a true gentleman Fargo had come to like, caught up in a war Fargo couldn't understand. After a moment, he finished his cheroot, dropped enough coins on the table to pay for both of them, and left the restaurant. He'd told the lieutenant earlier that this meal was on him—his contribution to the Confederacy.

* * *

34

Night had fallen over the town like a cool blanket. Fargo knocked on Ma Toady's door. Ma herself opened it, dressed in a black velvet dress that blended with the dark hallway, making her appear more enormous than she actually was—a neat trick. She stepped back to let Fargo in, a frown on her wide, pasty face.

"I don't want no trouble now, Fargo," she told him, remembering instantly Fargo's last whiskey-besotted visit.

"I'm not here to carouse, Ma," Fargo told her.

Ma shut the door. Two pale creatures slunk into view at the other end of the hall. The girls stood so as to allow their long black lace robes to swing open. Fargo glimpsed two dark triangles and a pair of ample breasts. With a grin, the girls closed off the view. Both were smoking cheroots and holding glasses. Fargo recognized one of them vaguely.

"Get back in there, girls," Ma said. "You know that ain't proper."

With a careless shrug the girls vanished.

"I'm looking for someone, Ma. Her name is Donna Alvarez."

"She's gone."

"Worked for you, did she?"

"She was here when you was, last time. I'm surprised you don't remember her."

"Where is she now?"

"Beats the shit out of me, Fargo. Last I knew she went over to that new parlor house opened up down the street, Fancy Anne's. Then I heard she picked herself a real tough nut to crack and got her ass whipped. She's gone, last I heard."

"Gone? Where?"

"Don't know."

"Thanks, Ma."

Her manner softened. "No need for you to be a stranger, Fargo," Ma said. "You're a real fine sporting man when you go easy on the sauce."

"If that's a compliment, I'll take it," Fargo said, opening the door. Tipping his hat to Ma, he stepped out into the cool night.

It was a short walk to Fancy Anne's parlor house, and from the look of it, Fargo understood why Ma Toady was so pleasant to him all of a sudden and why she was putting her girls up to behavior a lot more enticing and a just a little improper. She had competition. Fancy Anne's place was bigger than Ma's—a lot bigger—the veranda steps more solid and there was a cheerful red light at the windows. When he knocked on the door, it was opened by a small black girl in a starched apron and dress who greeted him with an immediate, bright smile.

"I'd like to see Miss Anne," Fargo told her.

"Why, come right in, sir," the maid said happily, closing the door after him and curtsying quickly. "I'll go get Miss Anne."

"Never mind," said a quiet, husky female voice. "I'll see to our guest myself."

Fargo turned to see a tall, golden-haired beauty stepping into the hallway from the parlor.

The black girl hurried off.

Her hand extended, Miss Anne approached

Fargo. "It's early," she told him. "But as I gather, you have been on the trail for some time." She smiled at his surprise. "I watched you ride in earlier," she explained. "I like a man who buys fresh clothes and visits a barbershop first thing."

Fargo introduced himself as he grasped Miss Anne's firm hand. She shook his with the firmness of a man, but there was little that was masculine in her eyes or in the fullness of her figure. It was enclosed in a tight-fitting dark-red dress with a white collar at her throat and a flaring splash of white lace at the bottom of her skirt. Her waist was as thin as a wasp's, but her high, melonlike breasts were more than a handful. And there was an incandescence in the madam's cheeks that aroused Fargo's interest and caused him to wonder if perhaps there might be times when she found an opportunity to play as well as work.

Still holding on to his hand, Miss Anne drew him after her into the parlor, where her girls were waiting. He saw the light jump into the eyes of those lounging on the settees and couches—and in one fiery redhead in particular. She had been on her way down the stairs and had halted the moment he entered.

"Girls," said Miss Anne, "meet our first customer of the evening, Skye Fargo."

They all smiled and headed for him. Fargo looked at Miss Anne. "If you're not too busy, I'd like a word or two with you—first."

"With me?"

"It's about Donna Alvarez."

Miss Anne's eyebrows went up a notch, and Fargo saw the redhead on the stairs draw back, her face suddenly alert, her eyes narrowing. Donna Alvarez was obviously more than just a name to this girl.

"In that case," Miss Anne said, "come with me."

She led Fargo from the parlor and down a narrow, thickly carpeted corridor to a door that led into her small office. Seating herself behind her neat desk, she smiled across it at Fargo, who was slumping his tall figure into an easy chair.

"Donna Alvarez is gone," Miss Anne said.

"Do you have any idea where?"

"To hell, I hope."

"You mind telling me why?"

"Do you mind telling me why you are asking for her?"

"Not at all."

Fargo briefly recounted the circumstances of Walt Tennyson's death and his dying request to Fargo. "So you see," Fargo said, finishing up, "I made a promise—one I intend to keep."

"You're a silly romantic, Mr. Skye Fargo. Donna is not worth a cent of that poor man's share."

"Would you care to explain that?"

"She ran off with one of my best customers. He boasted of a gold strike somewhere in the mountains north of here, and I am sure Donna was anxious to help him spend his millions. As you can imagine, it raised hell with the rest of my girls. Now they too are all looking for a man with a gold mine to take them away."

Fargo smiled. "I can't say as I blame them."

Miss Anne shrugged. "Perhaps not. But as you can see, Mr. Fargo, Donna Alvarez is no longer in need of your partner's share. That should be a relief to you and your other partners."

"I am sure it would—if I could let it go at that. You forget. I made a promise, more like a blood oath."

Miss Anne shook her head and got to her feet. "You men are all alike. You play at life the way a knight of old was supposed to do, all tied up with rules of conduct and complicated oaths of chivalry." She stopped beside his chair and smiled down at him.

"And all the while you women are laughing."

"Precisely, Mr. Fargo."

"When are you going to stop calling me *Mr.* Fargo?"

"When you and I break the rules of proper conduct. And go to bed."

Fargo got up. Again Miss Anne took his hand. This time she led him into a room off her office. It was her bedroom, lit by the soft glow of two amber-shaded lamps sitting on the dresser. The biggest item of furniture in the room was her canopied bed. Once she had drawn him inside the room, she closed the door and turned to face him, an almost impish smile on her face.

"As I said before," she told him, "I like a man who buys fresh clothes and visits a barbershop. You have no idea what some of these men smell like when they tramp in here looking for a lay, Mr.

Fargo. At such times, my girls would prefer their horses."

"I can imagine."

She smiled sadly. "No, I am afraid you couldn't—not unless you too have found yourself on your back, your legs spraddled while one of those whiskey-befouled animals panted over you."

Fargo frowned. The picture she painted for him was not a very pleasant one. "It must be almost enough to turn you against sex." He stepped closer to her.

"It is," she admitted, "until someone like you comes along."

They kissed then, her scalding tongue sending a fire racing through his groin.

Smiling, she pulled away. "Mmm, that was good. Get undressed while I go pour us drinks."

Fargo didn't argue with the lady. Shedding his clothes quickly, he hung his gun belt over the nightstand at the head of the bed, butt exposed, ready just in case. He was sitting on the edge of the bed, tugging on his boots, when Miss Anne returned, carrying a glass of what looked like champagne in each hand.

"You're a slowpoke," she commented, handing him a drink. Then she took a sip of hers and set it down on the dresser. "Here, let me help."

Fargo feasted his eyes on her while she tugged on his boots. All she had on now was a robe that hung open, allowing Fargo to gaze upon the softly rounded curves of her pink-tipped breasts, the taut-ness of her abdomen, the gentle swelling of her stomach and the blond, tufted triangle at the apex of her thighs. His boots off, she began to unbutton the fly on his pants. Reaching down, he cradled her breasts in his hands, squeezing them gently. She peeled off his trousers, then his long johns.

"Oh, my," she murmured when she saw his unrestrained erection spring up at attention. "You look like the best thing that's happened to me in a long time, Mr. Fargo."

Fargo pulled her to her feet, then bent his head to rub his lips over the budded tips of her breasts. He stopped long enough to say, "You look pretty good to me, also. Like you said, I been a long time on the trail."

He pulled her closer. She opened her thighs to straddle him, pressing her hips close to his and rocking against him urgently. Fargo kicked clumsily to get rid of the pants and underwear as Miss Anne clung to him, pressing down on his erection. He felt her moistness on him.

"About time we tried the bed," he told her.

"Wait! My drink," she cried, pulling free and hurrying back to the dresser. Watching her, Fargo finished his. She did the same, then ran lightly back to the bed. Just before she reached it, she turned slightly and fell backward onto the bed beside him, her arms lifting to him. He plunged down onto her, his lips closing hungrily about hers, while she hugged her to him with an embrace that almost strangled him.

"Mmm," she murmured as their lips worked frantically, "it's been such a long, long time. I'm more than ready, Mr. Fargo, but go into me slow—ever so slow. I want to feel every inch of you."

As she requested, Fargo took his time, letting himself plunge slowly into her until they were totally merged; then he drove in hard with a lunge that set Miss Anne to shuddering. Flinging her head back, she began breathing in short, ragged gasps.

"Don't move for a while yet," she pleaded. "Just wait a moment, please. I'm so close to letting go! But I don't want to—not yet!"

Fargo lay still, watching Miss Anne's face in the dim amber light. At last she relaxed and, with a nod, leaned back, a relaxed smile on her face. "Take me," she whispered. "All the way!"

He began to stroke, gently, steadily, Miss Anne keeping up with him, accepting his thrusts eagerly, a tiny cry of delight occasionally breaking from her. But gradually she became unable to contain her enthusiasm, breaking finally into a sudden frenzy of motion, twisting and heaving beneath him until he had to pin her with the full weight of his body. At last, the breath rushing from her throat in a long, expiring moan, she quivered one last time and lay still.

For several minutes she was silent, then sighed and said, "I disappointed you, didn't I?"

"Why do you say that?"

"Because you haven't come yet."

"Hell. I'm in no hurry."

"I tried to hold back. I really did. But I just had to let go. I could almost let go again right now, I've had to wait so long."

"Go ahead. Let go whenever you want," Fargo said, leaning gently forward and sinking his shaft still deeper into her.

"Mmm," she sighed, the red tip of her tongue moving along her upper lip. "Oh, my God! That feels so good."

He began thrusting a bit more urgently now, feeling the tip of his shaft nudging bottom. With an eager cry, Miss Anne brought up her legs and clamped them around his hips. He began stroking in earnest then, and after a couple of minutes Miss Anne went into another spasm of ecstasy, more prolonged than the last. Fargo slowed briefly, smiling down at her, then resumed his deep thrusting.

"Wait," she told him in a rush, "I want to you to go still deeper—deeper than you can go this way. Unless you—"

"Any way that pleasures, Miss Anne."

She thrust him eagerly off her. Fargo stood beside the bed while she grasped an ankle in each hand, then fell back, pulling her feet over her head. Fargo knelt in front of her and leaned forward. Releasing her ankles, Miss Anne let them rest on Fargo's shoulders, then grabbing his still-erect shaft eagerly, she guided it into her dripping crotch. He thrust urgently forward. She gasped, uttering a tiny keening cry of delight.

"Oh, that's it," she cried. "Now drive on in! Let me take every inch of you."

Fargo needed no further urging. Bracing his knees, he lunged forward, feeling himself go still deeper. Miss Anne began babbling incoherently within minutes, but he kept thrusting, feeling himself building to his climax now, but holding himself back until Miss Anne's throaty cries rose almost to a scream. He felt the muscles of her stomach contracting convulsively under his muscular belly and knew he could hold off no longer.

"Now!" she exclaimed. "Hurry! Hurry, Skye! Come with me this time."

Fargo let himself go. A powerful thrust or two more, and his body took over in a furious, steady rhythm that led swiftly to a quivering spasm that, when it came, matched hers almost perfectly. As his cock continued to pulse deep within her, he held himself hard against her soft body until they both stopped shuddering.

Uttering a deep sigh, Fargo rolled off her and watched as she stretched out her long legs, her eyes shut in contentment, a deep sigh escaping her.

There was a sudden knock on her office door.

"Damn," she muttered, rolling out of bed. "I told them not to disturb me."

Snatching up her robe, she vanished from the bedroom, pulling the door shut behind her. He could understand her irritation. He too had no desire to move from Miss Anne's bed. As a sweet lassitude fell over him, he reached out and took his Colt from its holster, thrust it under a pillow. With his trigger finger resting on the guard, he sank into a deep, satisfying sleep.

4

A light finger on his lips awakened him, and Fargo found himself looking up into the fathomless green eyes of the redhead he had glimpsed earlier on the stairs.

"Shhh!" she said, "Miss Anne send me in to comfort you, Mr. Fargo."

"Call me Skye," he told her.

She smiled and brushed a massive shock of red hair back off her freckled shoulders. "They call me the French girl." She grinned at him mischievously. "You know what that means?"

Fargo chuckled. "I reckon maybe I do, at that. What's your name?"

"Michelle."

"Get in here, Michelle," Fargo said, making room for her.

She stepped out of her gown and snaked in

eagerly beside Fargo, then snuggled close. "Now you must let me go to work."

"That what you call it?"

"With some men, yes, it is work. But I do not think it will be work with you. Miss Anne see the way I look at you when you come in. That is why she send me."

"She going to be away long?"

"A big party of miners come in, many with too much to drink. She think maybe she need to keep an eye on the men so they treat her girls nice."

"I see."

"Now you lean back and relax."

By that time her hands had closed about Fargo's exhausted plaything and found it as responsive as a large, wet noodle. She glanced up at him for a moment, her green eyes round with sorrow for him, and Fargo could see at once that she regarded his pitiable condition as a marvelous challenge. Eagerly, her head ducked back down and a second later he felt her hot hands stroking him while her hotter lips began blowing on the tip of his still-flaccid penis.

Fargo knew it was hopeless, but having no wish to disillusion the girl, he leaned back and let her have at him.

"You like doing that?" he asked.

"Oh, yes! I like to feel a man get hard in my mouth," she told him.

"Good luck."

"Don't worry. I not fail yet."

To his amazement, after a few minutes he felt his

penis growing erect, as if it had a life of its own. Soon, under her feverish yet expert ministrations, he was bigger than her hand. She closed her mouth eagerly about his slowly engorging mast, taking him shallowly at first, then going more and more deeply until his erection was such that she was forced to pull back and concentrate on the head of his thrusting cock. By this time he was beginning to move his thighs involuntarily under her as her expert tongue and lips played about the tip just under his foreskin with an expertise that threatened to drive him wild.

"Enough," he muttered gruffly, thoroughly aroused.

He was enjoying himself well enough, but he liked to take part. Taking Michelle by the armpits, he lifted her off his thigh. She resisted at first, as though reluctant to stop before bringing him to climax, but he brought her up bodily, held her above him until she opened her thighs, then plunged her down upon his erect shaft. She gasped as he plunged deep inside her, then she flung her head back and began to rock and sway lasciviously, grinding herself still farther down upon his rock-hard erection.

Her breasts were level with Fargo's mouth. He kissed their budded tips, taking them between his lips, caressing first one, then the other with his tongue, and occassionally nipping at them with his teeth. Each time he did this, Michelle shuddered with delight. Rocking wildly back and forth on his railroad spike, she flung her thick red hair from side to side, its tips brushing his knees.

Fargo was no longer holding back. Michelle's expert lips had done their job well. He began to thrust upward as the speed of her rocking gyrations increased and the tempo of her movements became spasmodic. She cried out—a long, keening wail— and Fargo brought his hips upward in a sustained thrust. Gasping, Michelle flung herself limply forward, entwining her arms about his neck.

"My God! It is I who am to arouse you. It is not for me to be aroused."

"Hell, why not?" growled Fargo, holding her close for a moment longer.

"I guess there is no reason." She sighed happily. "But for so long now I am paid to give others pleasure. It is almost a sin to find it oneself, do you understand?"

"No."

She stood up slowly and stepped back. "Stay there. I'll be right back," she told him.

She disappeared through the bedroom's rear door, and Fargo heard the muted clanking of a sistern pump. In a moment, she came back carrying a pan of water and a towel. Kneeling in front of Fargo, she proceeded to wash him off thoroughly, the water icily cold on his crotch. Finished, she placed the pan on the commode, then rejoined him on the bed, sitting up beside him, her head resting on his shoulder.

"Playing hooky?" he suggested with a laugh.

"Yes, maybe." Then she frowned. "I have question, Fargo."

"Shoot."

"Miss Anne say you ask about Donna Alvarez. Is that true?"

"It is."

"You know her from somewhere before this time?"

"Never laid eyes on her."

"That is strange."

"What can you tell me about her?"

"Miss Anne not know the truth. Only I know, because I see it. Donna Alvarez not go with this man because she want to—he force her."

"This man who took her. He have a name?"

"Bart Tobias."

"Can you describe him to me?"

"He is one big man with bald head and long, black mustache he wax very careful. On his head he wear, what you say—stetson?"

"Sounds right. What kind of horse does he ride?"

"A big gray gelding, I think."

"What's Donna look like?"

"Ah, she is what you say, perfect. Very dark hair, so long it goes to her waist. Her complexion, it is olive, and her eyes dark and liquid and the shape of almonds. She is very beautiful, most popular girl in the house, I can tell you."

"And you say this Tobias forced her to go with him."

She nodded vigorously. "When Donna try to fight

him that night, he beat her. So I try to help, but he beat me, too."

"And you didn't tell Miss Anne?"

Michelle sighed. "Donna and me, we not stay in Miss Anne's house that night. Instead, we sneak away to this man's hotel room. He promise me much gold if I do this, but I am afraid. So Donna, she come with me. When he see her, he forget all about me and take Donna."

"You mean you were going into business for yourself that night."

Michelle sighed and nodded unhappily. "This fellow, he promise so much gold if I do this thing. But now I think he have no gold. All he want is take woman with him. He is bad man. Terrible. I hope you will take Donna away from this man before he kill her."

Fargo sighed. After what Miss Anne had told him, he had just about written Donna Alvarez off. Now, he was not so sure. If Michelle was telling him the truth, Donna Alvarez needed his help—and Walt Tennyson's share of the gold—more than ever.

"Do you have any idea where this fellow took Donna?"

"North. Into the mountains. He say he have a map to mine, I think."

Fargo nodded wearily. It looked like he was in for a long journey into high country.

"Michelle! Come quick!"

One of Miss Anne's girls had stuck her head into the bedroom. Quickly, Michelle grabbed her gown and with a quick peck on Fargo's forehead, hurried from the room. Before she ducked out the door, she turned to him. "Please, Mr. Fargo. Do not forget poor Donna Alvarez!"

Then she vanished.

Fargo didn't wait for Miss Anne to return. It was a busy night, obviously. But a few minutes later, as he was pulling the outside door open, Miss Anne left the group she was entertaining and hurried out to bid him good night.

Fargo turned to her. "Thanks, Anne—for you and for Michelle."

Anne's eyes twinkled. "I knew you'd appreciate her. Come again, Skye."

He grinned at her. "After tonight, I may not be able to." He clapped on his hat and left.

Lt. Scott waved to his men. At once they set out, driving the horses before them. As a pall of dust lifted into the air, the lieutenant turned back again to Fargo and extended his hand. Fargo leaned over, the leather in his saddle squeaking, and shook it.

"This is an excellent gather of horseflesh, Fargo," the lieutenant said, smiling. "You and your men have done well. Are you absolutely certain you won't reconsider my offer?"

Fargo shook his head firmly. "Like I said yesterday, Lieutenant. Once was enough. Your best bet for more horses is California."

"Yes, I agree with you. And perhaps that is what we will have to do. All right, Mr. Fargo, good-bye and good luck. My compliments to your excellent crew."

With that Lt. Scott wheeled his big chestnut and rode out after his men.

Fargo sat his pinto for a while, watching the young officer until he vanished into the dust. Then he turned to his three remaining partners. They were watching him with an intensity that warned Fargo that his business with them was far from over. The gold had been divided into five equal shares, with Walt Tennyson's share going to Fargo. The grumbling had been bitter, but short-lived. Now, with the Confederate lieutenant gone, it was clear the three men were intent on making an issue of it.

"We'd like to talk to you," Yank said.

Fargo looked squarely at the beefy, horse-faced man and said, "The talking is done. You three got your share. Ride out."

"You can't get rid of us that easy," Clint said.

Tarnell, his broken nose swollen painfully, a purple bruise reaching up under one eye, moved his horse slightly to one side. He wasn't going for his gun again. He'd tried that once. But one of the others was about to take his shot, and if he did, Tarnell would be more than willing to jump in with both feet. From the sidelong glance Tarnell made at Yank, Fargo figured Yank would be the next one to try to put a bell on this here cat. That figured. It was early in the morning, yet Fargo could already smell the whiskey on his breath. Yank was all tanked up, filled with bravo juice, ready to make his move.

Fargo pulled his horse back and looked coldly at

Yank. "If you've anything you want to say, Yank, spit it out."

As Fargo spoke, his gun hand dropped so that the palm brushed lightly the grips on his Colt. Yank saw the move and swallowed. Beads of perspiration appeared on his long, narrow forehead. Fargo laughed as he saw the man's courage trickling away like piss down a rat hole.

But Yank had gone too far now to back down and went for his iron.

Fargo drew and fired in one silken-smooth motion, blasting Yank clear off his horse. The big man came down heavily on his back, a neat hole in his chest, his face the color of a dirty bedsheet. He kicked once, tried to say something, then settled on the rocky ground and died.

Fargo turned back to the other two, his Colt out now and probing the air like something alive, waiting. One look at the smoking bore and the two men backed their horses up hastily.

"You got your gold," Fargo barked angrily. "Ride out. Now."

The two men wheeled their horses and in a moment had disappeared beyond the cloud of dust they raised. Fargo didn't get down from his pinto. Instead, he glanced up at the sky. A buzzard was already circling, and soon there would be others.

He spurred northward toward the mountains, leaving whatever gold Yank had not spent on the dead man. Let the buzzards have the damn gold, he thought, he had too damn much already.

5

A week later, well into the mountains, Fargo was riding alongside a narrow stream when he saw a ranch house about a half-mile farther on. He brightened at once. He would appreciate some fresh coffee and maybe some bacon and thick slabs of homemade bread—if the owner of the place offered him a chance to light and set a spell, that is.

In order to reach the ranch house, Fargo found himself riding through the shadow of a high bluff parallel to the stream. A chill fell over him, one caused not by the coolness in the shadow, but by Fargo's sudden, sure knowledge that he was in danger. The hairs on his neck rose; he snapped his head to the right and glanced up. Kneeling on the lip of the bluff high above him was the dark silhouette of a rifleman.

Instantly, Fargo swung his pinto about and charged toward the base of the bluff. The rifleman fired, the round plowing a furrow in the ground behind the pinto's flying hooves. A second later Fargo was well in under the bluff, out of sight of the bushwhacker—a few scraggly pines shielding him from the rim. Dismounting swiftly, the Trailsman snaked his Sharps from his scabbard, saw to its load, then dug his way up the bluff's steep incline.

He was almost to the top when a second shot came at him from the rim, this round pounding into the bank just in front of Fargo's face. The explosion of dirt and rocks nearly blinded him. He flung himself flat beside a pine, blinked away the dirt, and brought up his rifle. This last shot had come from the bluff also, but from an entirely different emplacement, which meant he was being fired upon by two men. Twisting his head around so he could see the rim, he could find no target. He didn't like his situation. He was caught in the crossfire between two men—and he had no doubt who those two men were and what it was they wanted.

Fargo counted slowly to five, then turned about and, head down, charged out from behind the pine and up the steep slope. Bullets whined past him, but he kept his head and ass down until he was able to duck into a thick patch of brush close to the bluff's rim. Once he was out of sight, the rifle fire ceased. Fargo slipped on up through the brush until he reached the rim. Tall grass covered the tableland, and Fargo moved through it like a great snake, soon leaving the brush and the rim behind.

Not until he had covered at least fifty yards did

he pull up. Poking his head cautiously out through a thick patch of bunchgrass, he peered back at the rim. Not only did he see Clint Whitman and Slats Tarnell, but a few yards beyond them, sitting their horses patiently, five horsemen. Fargo muttered a curse. He should have figured the two men wouldn't have had the sand to go after him alone. Four of the riders had the hard, emotionless faces of hired gunslicks, each of whom, at the moment at least, seemed content to let Clint and Slats play out their hand.

The fifth rider was a woman.

She sat in the midst of these four waiting horsemen astride a powerful roan—a tall, broad-shouldered, hatless girl with long wheat-colored hair and a bosom that swelled opulently beneath the black woolen man's shirt she wore. Her wrists were bound to the saddle horn, and the entire lower portion of her face was wrapped brutally with a black bandanna to prevent her from crying out.

By this time Clint Whitman and Slats Tarnell had moved closer to the edge of the bluff, and Fargo watched as they peered down at the spot on the slope where they had last seen Fargo. A grim smile on his face, Fargo pulled himself cautiously around through the thick, waist-high grass, coming at the nearest to the two—Clint Whitman—from the rear. He was in no hurry as he measured his progress in inches. When he was close enough to chance a shot, he carefully shoved his rifle ahead of him, spread a a handful of linen cartridges on the ground beside it, then drew his Colt. Checking the Colt's load, he put it back down and picked up the Sharps.

The four riders were a good thirty to forty yards back. They were alert but relaxed, and none of them had their weapons out. Slats Tarnell was farther along the rim of the bluff, crouching beside a large boulder. The moment Fargo opened up on his former partners, those waiting four riders would charge him. But nothing would hold Fargo back now. He wanted these two sons of bitches, and he was going to get them.

Lifting his Sharps, Fargo sighted carefully on Whitman and squeezed the trigger. The man was still peering over the rim of the bluff when the bullet slammed into his ribs and sent him toppling forward and out of sight. Instantly, Slats Tarnell swung about, managed one quick snap shot at Fargo, then scrambled to get behind the boulder. Fargo lifted his Colt and fired twice. One .44 slug caught Slats somewhere high in the back and slammed him facedown into the ground. Fargo was hoping he might have finished the man until Slats roused himself and dragged himself out of sight behind the boulder.

By now the waiting horsemen were in action. They moved at full gallop across the tableland toward Fargo's prone figure, their six-guns blazing. Fargo slipped a cartridge into the Sharps' firing chamber and swung to his left to face them. As their rounds snicked through the grass around him, Fargo centered the sights of his Sharps on the lead rider and squeezed the trigger. The big slug caught the horseman full in the chest, knocking him back off his horse. At once the other riders spread out. But they kept coming. Fargo managed one more shot with his Sharps, but it missed. Snatching up his Colt, he tracked the closest rider, hoping for the best, and fired. The rider kept coming. Fargo fired again and this time caught the horseman in his right thigh. The man cried out and peeled off his mount.

That left two more riders, each thundering much closer now, and each with clear shots at him. It was time to take cover. Holstering his Colt, Fargo snatched up his Sharps and the remaining cartridges, turned, and raced back toward the brush along the rim. Bullets whined angrily past his head, and like a turtle, he tried to pull it in. The pounding of the horses' hooves grew louder with each passing second. The ground under his running feet trembled.

Determined not to take a bullet in the back, he held up suddenly and flung himself about, ready to throw his Colt up for one last shot, when he saw the blond girl astride her roan overtake the two riders and cut deliberately in front of them. Her horse smashed into the nearest rider, then swerved and caught the other rider's horse as well. In an explosive tangle of legs and horseflesh, all three horses and riders went down.

Reversing himself, Fargo raced back to the tangle of legs and manes. One of the riders fired at Fargo from the ground. Fargo returned the fire with his Colt, and the man lost his gun along with a few fingers. Frantic, he dragged his horse to its feet with his other hand and flung himself back into his saddle. The other one, still dazed from the collision, mounted up also, and the two horsemen rode off. Farther back, the rider Fargo had caught in the thigh managed to scramble back up onto his horse. Without a look back, he rode raggedly after his companions. Fargo threw one more shot at the fleeing riders, then ran over to the blonde's crumpled figure.

He was astonished. She had spurred her horse after the other riders, had managed to overtake them, and then flung herself and her mount in their path. He had seen her come down on top of one of the men, and it had appeared to Fargo that for a moment there she had been punishing furiously one of the downed riders with her fists.

Yet, all this time, her two hands had remained bound together.

He knelt by her side. She was unconscious, but breathing regularly. Fargo took out the bowie strapped to his leg and sliced through the rope binding her wrists. Then he began rubbing her hands together to restore circulation. She stirred and gasped slightly. Reaching down, he untied the bandanna still wrapped about her face and turned her head so she could see him when she awakened. She opened her eyes dazedly and glanced up at him, and Fargo found himself looking down into eyes as blue as the sky stretching above him and sensuous lips as fresh and red as ripe strawberries. Her most striking feature, however, was the dimple in the midst of her solid chin.

"You're alive," she gasped softly, pleased. "They didn't get you."

"No, they didn't. Thanks to you."

"I did what I could. It was not much."

"It was plenty."

"Who are you, anyway?"

"Skye Fargo. And you?"

"I'm Randy Swenson."

"What happened? Why were you with these men?"

"They stormed into my cabin this morning. They wanted to use the ranch as a trap for you. But I refused."

"So they bound you up?"

"They did worse than that—then decided to bushwhack you from this bluff."

"They knew I was coming?"

"They'd been trailing you for days."

Fargo nodded unhappily. He should have been more careful, more alert, he realized. "Stay here," he told her. "I want to look around, make sure none of them are on their way back."

She nodded.

Reloading his Sharps, Fargo trotted quickly over to the boulder behind which Slats Tarnell had dragged himself. He expected to find a dead man lying there or, at the very least, a severely wounded one. Instead, he found only the distinct, bloody path Tarnell's heavy body had made as he pulled himself through the brush.

Following the wounded man's spoor, Fargo came finally to a small clearing where he found Clint Whitman's horse tied to a sapling. Another horse had been standing beside Whitman's. It wasn't difficult for Fargo to figure out what had happened. Slats Tarnell had managed to pull himself up onto his own mount and ride off. Fargo opened the saddlebags that remained on Whitman's horse. They contained no gold dust, no trace of his share. Wounded though he was, Tarnell had delayed his flight long enough to take the gold from his partner's saddlebags. Sticky traces of blood showed on the pommel of Whitman's saddle.

Leaving Clint's horse, Fargo returned to the benchland and checked on the rider he had caught in the chest. The grass under him was already slick with the man's blood, his eyes staring sightlessly up at the sky, flies already swarming busily over his chest wound. Fargo glanced up. Vultures were circling overhead. A moment later, peering over the bluff's rim, Fargo saw Clint Whitman's sprawled figure lying near the stream far below. It had been a long drop, and the man was motionless.

He was dead enough, Fargo concluded.

Turning away from the rim, he hurried back to the girl. She was still on the ground, her mount back on its feet now and placidly cropping the grass some distance away.

"Can you get up?" he asked her.

"I think so," she said, and started to push herself erect. But at once she grimaced and with a small, startled cry of pain, fell back.

He went down on one knee beside her. "What's the matter?"

"I think I cracked one of my ribs."

"You live near here?"

"Yes, that ranch house beyond the bluff."

He nodded. It wasn't going to be easy getting her down there. He'd have to carry her, and each step would be torture for her. She wore dark woolen men's britches; he saw no sign of a corset or any petticoats under her shirt.

"I'll have to rip up your shirt," he told her, "and use it to bind your ribs while I carry you to the ranch. Will that be all right, Randy?"

Her face flushed. "Do what you have to, Mr. Fargo," she told him, her voice curiously light. He caught something devilish dancing in her eyes.

"All right, then," he said. He unbuttoned her shirt, pulled it gently off her, and ripped it into strips. She made no effort to cover her naked breasts as she lay on the ground before him, watching. When Fargo pulled her to a sitting position and began to bind her tightly about the rib cage, cold sweat from the pain broke out on her pale forehead, but she didn't utter a sound.

Fargo was perspiring too, only it wasn't caused by pain. Every time his big hands touched her warm, silken breasts or brushed one of her nipples as he snugged the strips of torn cloth more securely up under her bosom, he felt a tingle of excitement. It annoyed him slightly that he should be so susceptible to this woman's nearness. After all, this was no time for sport. The woman had been sorely injured.

Nevertheless, he could tell from the faint flush that spread across her cheeks that she too was caught up in the same excitement.

When he finished, he leaned back from her. "How's that feel?"

She smiled and looked past her nakedness at the snug bandage that bound her ribs. She moved one of her breasts aside. "Yes, that feels a lot better now. I can breathe more easily."

"What's the best way down to your place?"

"That way," she said, pointing carefully at a steep game trail that began some distance farther along the bluff's rim. "But we'll have to be careful."

"I'll carry you down first, then come back for your horse."

She nodded in agreement.

Taking her carefully in his arms, Fargo stood up, her fabulous, melonlike breasts lolling against his shirtfront just inches under his chin. She snugged her head against his shoulder and wrapped both arms tightly about his neck.

"Am I too heavy?" she asked.

"No," he told her—and in fact she did seem miraculously light. "What about you? Are you comfortable?"

"Mmm," she said softly, holding him still closer. "Yes, I am. Very."

He started off toward the trail she had pointed out to him, his senses reeling dangerously.

His senses were still reeling—as much from the

long climb down from the bluff under the hot sun as from his constant contemplation of Randy's charms. Mounting the porch steps with her in his arms, he had to be careful not to stumble, so befogged had his senses become. Even worse for him had been his contemplation of her erect, cherry-red nipples. Each time his eye caught one of them, his knees went weak with desire. As he stepped at last into her kitchen, his clouded senses were brought back to earth by the earthy smell of woodsmoke and fresh-baked bread.

Randy tightened her arms about his neck. "My bedroom's in the next room," she told him, her hot sweet breath nearly incinerating his ear.

Carrying her into it, Fargo found himself in a pleasant, almost radiant oasis. Sheer lavender curtains hung on the bedroom's two windows, the wall was recently whitewashed, and on it two lithographed landscapes were hung. Between the two windows sat a fine oak dresser with a large oval mirror, and spread neatly atop it were the girl's amber-colored comb-and-mirror set, some unguents, a music box with a dancing sprite on its lid, powder boxes, and rose water.

But it was the bed that dominated her room. It was a huge, canopied four-poster set luxuriously high off the spotless floor. Its canopy and bedspread were of the same shade of lavender as the curtains. The pillows were full and obviously packed with feathers.

Gently, Fargo lowered Randy onto her bed. When he tried to straighten, however, he found he couldn't. She refused to untwine her arms from around his neck. Instead, she increased her pressure and pulled Fargo down beside her on the silken coverlet. As she moved over to give him room beside her, she fastened her lips to his and Fargo found his senses reeling dangerously once more.

But alarm bells were ringing deep within him. This woman had been seriously hurt. She had one, possibly two, broken ribs. In addition, there was no telling what other internal injuries she might have suffered. That pileup she had engineered had been fearsome, and she was lucky to have come out of it as well as she had.

Gently, Fargo disengaged Randy's arms from around his neck and stood up, aware of his hat rolling down his back to the floor and of his inability to take his eyes completely off Randy's great, lolling breasts, their tips now stone-hard and erect.

"Now, just hold it right there, Randy," he protested. "You've sure as hell got me stoked up some. And once I start to burn, it'll take more than a summer shower to put me out. But, dammit, you've been hurt fearful, and what we're leading up to here is bound to call for some lively bucking. But I sure don't intend to hurt you any further."

"My, what a long speech," she said, smiling impishly up at him.

"I mean it, Randy."

"Now, look here," she told him, the tiny dimple in her square chin growing deeper with resolve. "I ought to know what I can do and what I can't. And Mr. Fargo, I'm not about to let this opportunity pass me by. My pa's off to Pine Top for supplies, and right at the tail end of a long, dull summer a man like you shows up!"

In spite of himself, Fargo smiled. "I'm just thinking of your condition, Randy."

"Well, then," she said, a sudden, imperative gleam in her eyes. "Think of my condition then. I'm all fired up and raring to go. You got all your teeth, you got shoulders as wide as a barn door, you don't smell like cow or horse manure, and you got real pretty eyes—almost like mine. Beside all that, I can tell you're a gentleman."

"Not all the time," Fargo warned her.

"Good! Now you just get back down here and snuggle close. You won't hurt me none. I won't let you. Just be careful is all. Real careful." She smiled then, a dazzling smile. "You can do that, can't you?"

"But, Randy, you're hurt."

"I'll be hurt a damn sight worse if you don't stop all this fool palavering and get back down here where you belong."

Fargo shrugged and began to unbutton his shirt. At once, in a fever of impatience, Randy leaned over, tugged Fargo down onto the bed beside her, and began unbuttoning his fly. He did what he could to help her, aware as always that it was a lot more dangerous to turn a woman down when she wanted to play than it was to force a woman who didn't.

In a gratifyingly short time, there were no further impediments between himself and Randy's long, silken-smooth body—except, of course, for the strips of Randy's shirt still bound tightly about her ribs. Careful not to cause her any pain, he concentrated first on warming her up, starting with kisses, then with long, affectionate attention to her breasts, his tongue flicking at her erect nipples while his light, caressing hand explored the rest of her body completely.

Only when Randy began to moan aloud did he carefully spread her out before him, ease himself up onto her, and then—with exceedingly great care—enter her.

Randy gasped. "My God, Fargo," she cried, "you know how to drive a woman wild. And so far it doesn't hurt at all!"

He grinned down at her. "Now just lie quiet, Randy, and let me see what I can do."

She closed her eyes and nodded.

He was mildly astonished at the ease with which he penetrated her. So moist had she become as a result of the extended attention he had given her beforehand that at first he could barely feel himself inside her. But quickly the walls of her vagina tightened about his erection with the force of a powerful fist, and he felt himself swell magnificently inside her as he began eagerly probing her warm depths.

At first, he moved almost fearfully, but after a few urgent thrusts, his desire outstripped his concern, and he began plunging with greater and greater abandon. He heard Randy gasp in pleasure, turned his head, and buried his lips on hers. Her mouth opened eagerly as their tongues found each other in an embrace as passionate as their own. Meanwhile, he kept thrusting, and with each additional probe, he plunged still deeper into her warm moistness, his fear of hurting her vanishing entirely as he felt her pelvis rocking up hungrily to catch each of his own downward thrusts.

"Fargo!" she called softly to him, her head suddenly flung back, her eyes still closed tightly. "You're in so deep, I can taste you. I swear it!"

"Shh . . ." he told her, increasing the pace of the rhythmic thrusts. "Just lie still and enjoy it."

She did as she was told. By now Fargo was mounting inexorably to his own climax. He made a valiant effort to hold back, not sure about Randy and not wanting to hurt her, but found himself unable to temper his passion. Caught up completely now, he swept past the point of no return and was pounding toward his orgasm when he heard her gasps, then her sharp, inarticulate cries. He thought she was screaming, and wasn't sure whether to stop or go on. But he was no longer in control, no longer the concerned gentleman. Then, just as Fargo reached his own, shattering, pulsing climax, Randy came also, thrashing her head back and forth and uttering a high, keening scream.

Fargo pulled himself free and quickly rolled off Randy. "Are you all right?" he asked, his voice filled with genuine concern.

She turned her head to look at him, a lazy smile on her face, her blue eyes lidded with smoky passion. Stretching lazily, she nodded. It was obvious her fires were not yet entirely quenched.

"I'm fine," she told him. "Just fine. That was worth waiting all summer for. Now get back over here. That was a nice beginning, but we've got the rest of this day and then there's tonight."

"But your ribs!"

"You know what?" She smiled again as she reached down with her hand to fondle him. "I think they're already beginning to knit together. If they get any worse, you can always bandage me up again, can't you?"

He smiled back at her. "All right, but now I think I'd better go bring in our horses. It'll give me time to recover. Think you can wait that long?"

"I'll try," she said, pushing her lower lip in what passed for a pout.

He laughed and slipped from the bed. As he dressed, he found himself hurrying, anxious to return to Randy. Maybe she was right. This kind of activity might be just the thing to help her ribs heal a bit faster. One thing was for certain: it was cheering her up something fierce—and doing him a hell of a lot of good besides.

The next morning, a tight corset serving as a brace for her cracked ribs, Randy was standing at the stove, humming softly as she prepared Fargo's breakfast. She was barefoot, and over the corset she wore an apron. And that was all. There was nothing under the apron's straps, not even a chemise, only her long, bare, silken legs.

Watching her at the stove as he entered the kitchen, Fargo marveled at the woman's beauty and even more at her stamina. Less than an hour before, awakening him with a kiss, she had prevailed upon him once again and had somehow managed to extract from his depleted groin the last full measure a kind Providence had left within him.

He was pleasantly drained. A few minutes before, when he had checked outside, he had had the odd feeling that the first strong wind would be enough to waft him away like some insubstantial dandelion seed. Pushing his holster out of the way now, he sat down at the table and looked over the woman before him. He needed this breakfast she was fixing for him, needed it badly. Satisfying the needs of this extraordinary Norse maiden, who had been forced to wait far too long between lays, wasn't the only reason he was in this country—no matter what she might think.

Leaning over him maddeningly, she brought him his bacon and eggs and fries and thick, buttered slices of homemade bread. As she placed the meal down before him, the warmth of her nearness almost overpowered him, especially when he happened to glance into the cleft between her magnificent, incandescent breasts.

He forced himself to look back at the food Randy had placed down before him. But she was an incorrigible tease. When she sat down across from him, she leaned forward on her folded arms, supposedly to watch him eat, exposing her full breasts almost completely. To his amazement, as he reached for the buttered bread, he felt himself growing larger.

He caught her gleaming eye then, and she laughed, delighted.

"You're a witch," he told her. "I swear."

"No, I'm a woman."

"No difference."

"Perhaps you're right."

The bantering conversation caused him to relax. He said, "Now tell me. Who were those four men?"

"Jim Clements is their leader. Hank Mitchum and Silas Swallow were the other two. I don't know the fourth rider's name—the one you shot out of the saddle."

"He's dead anyway. I don't have to worry about him anymore."

"They're known as the Clements gang. They've been tearing up the territory for more than a year now. They're worse than Apaches."

"What did they know about me?"

"Only what your partners told them, that you were carrying two saddlebags filled with gold. They said it was their gold and that you had stolen it from them."

"Did you believe that?"

"No. And neither did that gang. Those two partners of yours sure were fools to throw in with that pack of hyenas. As soon as they got your gold, they would have slit your partners' throats and taken off with all of the gold."

Fargo nodded. He had checked to make sure the pouches containing his gold dust were still resting inside his saddlebags. At the moment the saddlebags were on the floor in the corner of Randy's bedroom.

His breakfast finished, Fargo leaned back and reached for his coffee. He felt like a new man, as light as a feather and fit as a fiddle. A woman could do that for a man, he realized. And now, looking across the table at Randy made him feel even better.

Suddenly the kitchen door swung open, and Clint Whitman's bloody, disheveled figure loomed crookedly in the doorway, a six-gun in his hand. "You son of a bitch," he rasped hoarsely. "Thought I was dead, didn't you? That creek saved me. I spent all night crawling to this place. Now I got you dead to rights."

Whitman was hatless. His bloodied chest was matted with grass and dirt, his Levi's heavy and stiff with dried blood. An awesome stench hung about the man and quickly filled the kitchen. He must have fouled himself during the night. His eyes, tight with pain, peered at Fargo out of a face the color and texture of a dirty bedsheet.

"You're hurt, Clint," Fargo told him, getting to his feet. "Put down that gun."

"Not till I've finished with you, Fargo."

"Don't be a fool. You need to see a doctor—not an undertaker."

Whitman straightened his heavy figure, his gun hand shaking dangerously. "You can't talk your way out of this," he told the Trailsman. "I don't care about gold now. All I want is to nail your ass."

Fargo knew there was a chance that the Clements

gang might return, so powerful a magnet was gold. But he hadn't figured on Clint Whitman's bullet-riddled body rising from the dead, a six-gun in his hand and death in his eyes.

"There's just one thing, Clint," Fargo told the man, stepping out from behind the table. "This girl here had nothing to do with our trouble. When you kill me, go easy on her."

Clint shook his head doggedly. "No," he said thickly. "I'm going to kill her, too." He coughed raggedly. A thin tracery of blood left the corner of his mouth. "Any friend of yours is no friend of mine."

"You mean I can't talk you out of it?" Fargo said, taking another step away from the table. "You won't put down that gun?"

Clint peered wearily at him and moistened his cracked lips. "No," he managed. "I won't. I'm going to kill you now." Raising his six-gun a notch higher, Clint cocked it.

In one smooth motion Fargo drew his Colt and fired, then cocked and fired again. Two fresh holes appeared in Clint Whitman's chest. The man rocked back, astonishment registering on his beefy face. He hadn't even seen Fargo draw. As his knees collapsed under him, he lowered his gun and squeezed the trigger, the big gun thundering in the small room as it blasted a hole in the floor.

Then he tipped slowly over like a broken toy.

6

It was after ten that morning when Fargo finished his grisly task.

He buried Clint first, then went looking for the rider he had shot from his horse the day before. He found him on the bluff where he'd left him, surrounded by a full congregation of vultures ready for the feast. The big, ungainly birds had been a bit testy at the prospect of losing their meal, but Fargo had waded in among the humpbacked diners, flailing his spade with mean precision. So sluggish had their gluttony made them, they had difficulty lifting into the quiet, morning air.

Fargo had buried the gunslick where he lay, and now, leaning wearily on the spade's handle, he lit a cigar, grateful for the smoke's ability to banish the stench of death. His smoke finished, he flung away the cigar stump and returned to the farmhouse.

He found that Randy's father had returned. The man was standing with his daughter on the front porch as Fargo approached. Randy introduced Fargo to her father as the man who had saved her from the Clements gang, and Fargo received a hearty, grateful handshake. His name was Matt, and he was a tall, rugged blond of about forty years, as strikingly handsome as his daughter was beautiful. They made a fine-looking father and daughter.

"If there's anything I can do to help you, Fargo," Matt said, escorting Fargo into his ranch, "just say the word."

"As a matter of fact, maybe you can. I'm looking for two people. A man and a woman. The man's name is Tobias, Bart Tobias—and the girl's name is Donna Alvarez."

"Maybe you could describe them some," Matt suggested as the two men sat down at the deal table while Randy fetched the jug of moonshine she kept under the sink.

Having to rely solely on Michelle's description of them, Fargo didn't have an easy time describing the two, but he did the best he could. Matt was bemused at Fargo's reason for wishing to locate Donna Alvarez, but made no attempt to belittle his quest, obviously respecting Fargo's determination to keep his promise to a dying man.

His brows knit in concentration, Matt said, "As a matter of fact, when I hit Pine Top about a month ago, I saw a couple that reminds me of the two you just described. The woman was Spanish, all right, and a real fine-looking filly. She was sitting up on a wagon seat. The fellow with her had just finished purchasing supplies. They were heading into the mountains west of Pine Top, as I recall. The reason I took notice was the girl. A few minutes before they left town—I was just stepping out of the barber shop at the time—I saw the girl try to get away from this fellow. He went like a shot from a cannon and wasn't at all gentle as he dragged her back to the wagon."

"You think this man was Tobias?"

"In the struggle with the girl, his hat came off. And his black handlebar mustache was waxed solid."

"And no one tried to help the girl?"

"Hell, Fargo. Do you know anyone fool enough to get himself caught between a man and his woman? This fellow was a tough-looking hombre and carried a well-oiled hogleg strapped to his thigh. I got the distinct impression he knew how to use it. Besides, he rode out only a few minutes later."

"The man's horse. Was it a gray?"

"That's right. A big gray."

Fargo leaned back, pleased. He was getting closer. "And they were headed into the mountains west of Pine Top, you say?"

"It looked that way to me."

"And this was about a month ago."

"Yup."

Fargo poured himself another cup of the moonshine and threw it down his gullet, smacking his lips as it warmed his insides. A month was a long start and this was big country. A lot could have happened to those two in that time. But at least he had some idea of Tobias' location, and there was always the chance he would return to Pine Top for more provisions.

"Just steer me toward Pine Top, Matt, and I'll be off."

"What's the hurry?" Swenson protested.

Fargo smiled. "No hurry, but I've still got a long way to go."

"You don't need to explain," Matt said. "I like a man who keeps his promises. Damn few do."

Not long after, Fargo stepped into his saddle and looked down from the pinto at Randy and her father. The directions Matt had given him were clear enough. All he had to do was follow the stream until it broadened into a river, then keep going until he reached Pine Top. Matt advised Fargo it was a two-day ride if he took his time.

"Them Clements are likely to head for Pine Top, too," Matt warned. "There's a doctor there. Doc Gurney. He's pretty good at pulling bullets out of people. That's one reason the place attracts so many hard cases."

"I'll remember that."

Matt extended his hand up to Fargo. Fargo reached down and shook it. "If you're ever in this neck of the woods," Matt told him, "ride over and rest a spell. And next time stay longer."

"Yes," Randy said, shading her blue eyes as she moved up beside her father. "I sure do wish you'd do that."

"Thanks," Fargo told them, touching the brim of his hat in salute.

Then he wheeled his pinto and set out for Pine Top.

Two days later, close to nightfall, Fargo rode into the town. It was not much of a town, nor was there any trace of pine. The place was a collection of weathered, unpainted buildings and shacks clustered in under a ragged bluff. Fargo passed a general store, two or three cheap hotels, saloons, a mill, a couple of parlor houses, and a large, three-storied hotel called the Colonial House. It had seen better days, but was in pretty good shape, considering the company it was forced to keep.

Four of the saloons were clustered about the big hotel. The biggest one next to the hotel called itself the Miner's hole. As Fargo rode past it, a few bar girls peered out at him, their painted lips a livid contrast to their flat, sunless faces.

Perched on the porches of each saloon were the patrons, the noxious weeds that sprouted so readily from such bitter soil. A few sat on the porch flooring, their backs to the posts, while others lazed about on the tops of barrels or straight-backed chairs tipped back against the wall. Some whittled, others just sat . . . like crows on a branch. The only thing clean or well-kept about them were the holstered guns strapped to their thighs. All of the men were hard cases, and Fargo's sharp eyes noted each one—searching, always searching, for the two men he knew he would someday find.

The livery stable ran off a dank, side street within sight of the hotel. A fading sign that said HANK'S LIVERY was nailed over the door just under a rusty horseshoe. As Fargo dismounted and led his pinto into the barn, a one-legged ancient—his face almost hidden behind an unkempt beard—swung out of a small room on a single, battered crutch. As Fargo led the pinto into a clean stall, the old man clumped deftly after him without a word. The smell of horse manure was heavy in the place, reminding Fargo that a one-legged man probably had a difficult time wielding a pitchfork.

"You Hank?" Fargo asked the old-timer as he unsaddled his Ovaro.

"Yup."

Fargo peeled off the saddle blanket, rubbed the pinto's damp back dry, then stepped past the owner to fetch some oats and a bucket of water.

"That'll be fifty cents," Hank said.

"What for?"

"For the use of the stable and oats, mister. Ain't you never heard of a livery stable before?"

"Sure. But I'm doing all the work in this one."

"That's why it's so cheap, mister."

Fargo hesitated.

The old-timer grinned, showing great gaps where his teeth should have been. "You want I should sic some of them fellers out front on you for trying to cheat a cripple."

"Gee whiz, mister, don't do that." Then Fargo grinned and flipped the stable owner a coin. "I understand you got a good sawbones in this town."

Hank relaxed and pocketed the coin. "You mean Doc Gurney?"

"That's the one. Where'd I be likely to find him?"

"Doc's usually in the Miner's Hole—when he's got the price of a drink, that is."

"Thanks."

Fargo hefted his gold-filled saddlebags onto his shoulder and, carrying his Sharps, left the livery and crossed the now dark street to the hotel. He got a room on the second floor in front and decided to accept it when he saw that the veranda roof was an easy drop from his window. Then he went back down to explore the town—and maybe have a chat with Doc Gurney, if he could find him.

As soon as he started asking questions about the doctor, the patrons of the Miner's Hole gave Fargo a wide berth. Accepting this fact with a shrug, he took his bottle and glass to a table near the window and leaned back to wait. He was halfway through the bottle when he saw a pinched, shrunken man in a dusty black frock coat and black derby, carrying a small black instrument bag, push through the batwings and make a beeline for the bar. He ordered a bottle of rye and a glass and found a table in the rear. Placing his black instrument bag hurriedly down on an empty chair beside him, he poured and drank. Then he poured and drank again.

This, without a doubt, was Doc Gurney.

Fargo watched him for a while before getting up and carrying his bottle and glass over to the doctor's table. "Mind if I join you, Doc?"

The doctor looked blearily up at him. "You can sit anywhere you want. It's a free country."

"Much obliged."

"Don't thank me. Thank Thomas Jefferson."

Fargo sat down and made himself comfortable. The doctor ignored him completely and continued to gulp his rye, evidently celebrating the end of a prolonged dry spell. Abruptly, the man's eyes clouded and his face went slack; he let his head drop forward onto his arms and fell instantly asleep.

Fargo leaned back, drank slowly, and waited.

About a half-hour later the doctor stirred, lifted his head, and looked coldy at Fargo. "You still here?" he rasped, reaching for the rye bottle.

Fargo nodded.

"Who the hell are you, anyway?"

"Skye Fargo."

From the change in the sawbones' expression, Fargo could tell the man had heard his name before—more than likely from the men the doctor had just been repairing. The doctor looked carefully at Fargo. "What do you want? You got a bad case of piles, maybe?"

"Nope."

"Then what do you want with me?"

"Information."

Doc Gurney glanced quickly around the saloon, obviously looking for help. By this time a sizable crowd of patrons were holding up the bar, and at least four poker games were in progress. Heavy coils of blue smoke hung in the air above their tables, and a fresh crew of percentage girls were filtering through the crowd. Yet in all that crowd the doc didn't find one friendly face, it appeared, one man who might be willing to bail him out.

"Don't get nervous," Fargo told the doc. "You don't need any protection from me. I just want to know where Jim Clements and his boys are holed up."

The man looked warily at Fargo, like a small animal coming out of a hole in the ground. "What makes you think I'd know anything about them?"

"Your profession—and your reputed skill in extracting lead from assholes like Clements."

"What do you want with Jim Clements?"

"I want to know if he and his men are healthy enough to keep on after me. And don't tell me you don't know why I'm asking."

The doc leaned back in his chair. "Maybe I did hear mention of you, at that," he admitted.

"And the gold."

"Maybe that, too."

"Doc, I'd just as soon ride out of here without the crowd on my tail. So all I want from you is some estimate of their condition. I'm asking polite, but I could get nasty."

"I got friends in this town."

Fargo sighed. "Then you'd rather side with three cutthroats than an honest man."

The doctor shook his head. "How do I know you're any more honest than Jim Clements? How's a man get all that gold you're supposed to be carrying around if he's honest?"

"From hard work."

The doctor gave up sparring with Fargo. With a shrug, he reached for the bottle of rye. "Clements and the two others you shot are holed up in a hotel down the street."

"Two others?"

"You heard me. A fellow with half his hand shot off and another one with a bullet in his shoulder."

"I caught one of them in the thigh."

"That poor son of a bitch couldn't make it this far. So they left him."

"The one with the bullet in his shoulder. His name wouldn't be Slats Tarnell, would it?"

"If you know, what're you asking me for?"

"Does he know I'm in town?"

"Not yet." He bared his yellow teeth in what was supposed to be a grin. "But I wouldn't bet my life on him and Clements not finding out you're here pretty damn soon."

"Who's going to tell them? You?"

"You bet your ass. Next time I see them."

"All right. You do that. And when you do, tell them I got no hard feelings. I'm willing to let bygones be bygones. All I want is a chance to ride on without them buzzing around me. That's fair enough, isn't it?"

The doctor shrugged.

"Maybe you ought to go tell them now."

"I ain't finished this bottle yet."

"Finish it, and I'll buy you another."

The man's eyes lit at the prospect, and he set to work swilling down what was left in his bottle of rye. Before he got a chance to empty it, however, he had slumped forward onto his face and begun to snore softly.

Fargo left the table, purchased a fresh bottle of rye from the bartender, placed it down on the doc's table, and left the saloon.

Back up in his room, he peered into his saddlebags to make sure he was still solvent, then shoved them well in under the bed and checked his Colt's load. He figured it would take the doctor at least half an hour before he recovered his senses to hightail it back to Clements with the good news.

Bunching the pillow and bedclothes to make it appear he was sleeping in the bed, Fargo turned off the lamp on his dresser and lifted the shades to let in the moonlight. Then he strode to the doorway and looked back at the bed. He was satisfied. In the moon's pale light it looked as if he were sleeping peacefully.

Returning to the window, he sat down on the floor beneath it, his six-gun in his hand and his back to the wall. He hoped he didn't fall asleep before his guest arrived.

Perhaps an hour later, Fargo's head shot up as he heard a pair of heavy footsteps stealthily approaching his door. The last shreds of sleep vanished as the door was kicked open and a big man—Jim Clements, Fargo had no doubt—charged in, gun blazing.

The detonations rocked the room with a sound so thunderous Fargo could barely hear the slugs plowing into the mattress and pillows. As he peered through the gunsmoke, a second gunman—his right hand swathed in bandages—pushed into the room after Clements and added his fusillade. Neither of them saw Fargo or even glanced in his direction.

Fargo got off two quick shots and saw the man with the bandaged hand stagger and fall, while Clements, confused by this unexpected return fire, backed hastily out of the room. Fargo heard his heavy footsteps racing down the hallway.

Turning, Fargo flung open his window and dropped to the veranda roof. Like a big cat, he landed in the street just in front of the hotel in time to see Clements dash out of the hotel onto the veranda. When he saw Fargo, he was so astonished he delayed momentarily in flinging up his gun. Fargo didn't delay. Firing first, he caught Clements squarely in the gut.

Stopped cold in his tracks, the gunman dropped his weapon, clutched at his belly, and toppled down the steps. He landed facedown, his nose plowing up a manure-laden rut.

Fargo holstered his gun and walked over to examine Clements, a growing crowd at his heels. With his boot, he rolled the body over to see the man's face. Fargo had glimpsed Jim Clements only once during that shoot-out on the bluff near Randy's place, but it was enough. He recognized the face at once.

"Jesus," a hushed voice said behind Fargo. "That's Jim Clements."

"He's a goner," said another.

An angry murmur swept through the crowd.

Then a high, piping voice cried, "Someone get Doc Gurney."

Fargo looked around at the crowd. "Where's the law in this town?"

"You must be kidding, mister."

A second later Doc Gurney pushed his way through the crowd and knelt beside Clements. After a quick examination, he pronounced the gang leader dead.

"There's another one upstairs, Doc," Fargo told him. "In my bedroom."

"Is he dead?"

Fargo shrugged. "I didn't hang around to find out."

As the doc hurried into the hotel, Fargo followed after him, while the crowd of sullen men watched from the street. Glancing back, Fargo wondered how long it would be before they decided to take after the man who had just shot down two of their own.

The doc identified the other dead man as Hank Mitchum. After the corpse had been carted away, the desk clerk found Fargo a new room farther down the hallway, since the bed in his first room was now a smoking mass of pulverized feathers and sheets. Once Fargo was alone, he checked his saddlebags once again, then dragged the mattress off the bed and over to the wall beside the window. So far this night, he had taken care of two men hungry for his gold. But that still left Slats Tarnell. Tarnell's shoulder wound was probably what kept him from joining Clements and Mitchum in tonight's gunplay, but that didn't mean Tarnell wouldn't make his own move now, figuring Fargo would probably let his guard down after the shootout. It was, admittedly, a long shot, but Fargo couldn't afford to relax now.

He was sitting up on the mattress, reloading his Colt in the dim light filtering through the window, when someone knocked softly but firmly on his door.

Leveling his gun at the door, Fargo called wearily, "Come on in. The party's just beginning."

The door was pushed open, and into the dark, moonlit room stepped an older woman of considerable heft. She was dressed in a long, rose-colored, satiny nightgown. Though she was wearing a nightcap, her long hair—still gold, but streaked with gray—had been combed out so that it flowed well past her shoulders and down her back. Even in the dim light, Fargo could see that she had been a handsome woman in her prime, and could possibly still turn a few heads if she had a mind to do so.

When she saw the bare, gleaming bedsprings in the dim light, she looked startled. Glancing swiftly around, she caught sight of Fargo squatting on the mattress by the window, his six-gun pointed at her. Instantly, her confusion turned to outrage.

"Put that cannon down, mister, or I'll have you thrown out of this hotel. I'm an unarmed woman, and I didn't come here to be threatened."

"I wasn't expecting you, ma'am," Fargo said, dropping the Colt into his holster beside him on the floor. "I've had a bad night so far. Maybe you heard."

As Fargo spoke, he got to his feet. He was not wearing a shirt. She looked at him for a long moment, noting his build and the way he stood before her, and seemed to like what she saw. Her anger faded. She took a deep breath and smiled.

"I heard about your tribulations, mister," she told him. "This here's my hotel, and I've come up here to offer you some help."

"All the help I need, ma'am, is a good night's sleep."

"Well, you won't get that if Jim Clements had any friends in this town, and I'm afraid he did. Clements was a prime bastard, but he never shit in his own nest, and he paid his bills."

"What's your offer?"

"Come downstairs to my suite. As my guest, you'll be perfectly safe."

"That's right neighborly of you, ma'am, but won't that raise hell with your reputation?"

"Never had to worry about such nonsense, mister. Not in my line of work, if you get my meaning. I've retired these past years, but everyone in this part of the territory knows where I got the money to buy this hotel. Everybody knows and nobody cares."

"And you're sure I'll be safer down here than on this mattress?"

"Safer and a damn sight more comfortable."

"You're on, ma'am. I thank you kindly, and if

you'll wait just a minute, I'll get my gear and follow down after you."

"I'll wait."

It didn't take Fargo long to replace the mattress on the bed, grab his saddlebags and the rest of his gear, and follow after the woman as she led him down the stairs to her suite off the front desk. Fargo followed her into her suite and found himself in a spacious office, with a large bedroom off it. A lamp was lit in the bedroom, and the room radiated a feverish glow, since everything in it—including the drapes and coverlet—was either pink or red, a fit reminder of the hotel owner's previous line of work.

Closing the door behind him, the woman turned to Fargo and smiled. "My name's Beverly," she told him. "Beverly Smith, if you need a last name. And you'd be Mr. Fargo."

"Skye Fargo," Fargo told her, looking for a place to drop his things.

She pointed to a corner beside her desk. "Your gold will be safe over there," she told him, "and the rest of your gear."

"You know about the gold?" he asked, dropping the saddlebags in the corner she'd indicated.

"I know, and maybe half the territory knows besides."

Fargo winced and shook his head. He should have guessed it. Neither Whitman nor Tarnell was very good at keeping his mouth shut—and once Jim Clements and his boys were made privy to the information, Fargo might as well have published the news. The Trailsman had no doubt that in addition to Slats Tarnell, every trigger-happy punk in this territory would now be gunning for him. As he had noted earlier, gold was certainly a powerful magnet.

Beverly read his thoughts and laughed. "That's right, Mr. Skye Fargo. You're a famous man, carrying all that gold. And from what I hear, half of it is for a woman you've never seen."

"It's a long story, Beverly," he told her, "and I'm tired."

She shrugged and lifted a kerosene lamp from the desk and started into her bedroom. At the door, she paused and turned to him. "You can sleep in bed with me, or on the sofa over there."

"Would it hurt your feelings, Beverly, if I chose the sofa?"

"Not at all. I figured, from the look of you, that you'd refuse my invitation. Besides, even though I'm retired and all, it still goes against the grain to give it away. Old habits die hard, I guess."

Once Fargo was stretched out comfortably on the office sofa, he heard Beverly begin to snore. He got up and closed the door between the two rooms and dropped back onto the sofa and buried his head in a pillow, congratulating himself on his wisdom in turning down Beverly's invitation.

He would never have gotten to sleep alongside that awesome series of detonations.

7

Breakfast was brought in to them the next morning by a young Indian girl not much older than sixteen. Fargo was wearing only his buckskin britches, and Beverly looked cool and refreshed in a frilly pink bathrobe. And under that bathrobe, Fargo was pretty certain, there was nothing but Beverly.

They ate in a cozy nook in her bedroom, looking out through a modest bay window at Pine Top's streaming back alley. A series of dilapidated outhouses emptying into the noisome ditches were caught in the bright morning sun's first golden shafts. The ancient weathered face of the bluff that overlooked the town blazed forth next.

Beverly noted Fargo's sardonic gaze as he took note of the outhouses. She laughed softly, her opulent figure jiggling. Despite her size, she had a surprisingly pretty face, and her long hair, still combed out, had much to do with that. They were finishing off the breakfast with their second cup of coffee.

"Not much of a view, I admit," Beverly said, "but the other side's no better, I'm afraid. Horse tails swinging at hitch racks. Whiskey-sotted gunslicks with hogleg sitting on their asses, planning schemes that will lead them and fools like them to mean deaths." She sighed and smiled at Fargo. "I prefer my crooked line of outhouses out back here—and that distant bluff."

"How'd you come to settle here?" Fargo asked. "And even more important, how were you able to keep me from getting chewed up by those gunslicks out there? What prevented them from storming in here if they had a mind to do so?"

She smiled. "Any more questions?"

"One more. How come you took under your wing last night a man you never saw before in your life?"

"You wouldn't happen to have a cigar, would you?" she inquired.

Fargo left the table and pulled out a couple of cigars from his war bag. Slicing off the end of Beverly's, he lighted it for her, then lit his own. Beverly leaned back and puffed contentedly. As soon as the girl had finished clearing off the table, Beverly fixed her impish green eyes on Fargo and began to talk. She told him of her youth in Connecticut and of her strict Calvinist background that she constantly rebelled against.

At last, unable to endure any more of what her parents called a "strict, Christian up bringing," she ran off with a drummer, who of course dumped her first chance he got in a St. Louis hotel. Forced to take up the only profession a girl in her circumstances found open to her, she eventually reached Pine Top, by this time as a madam with her own complement of fresh young girls. While the gold and silver mines lasted, she put away enough money to buy this hotel. The mines had been played out for more than five years now, but she remained in Pine Top, satisfied that she had found a quiet place at last, a roof over her head, and an occupation that allowed her to sleep most nights.

Fargo nodded. It was, he realized, an old, old story—but for Beverly it had, so far, ended much better than it usually did for the soiled doves that took up this oldest of all the professions.

"Now," Beverly said, "as to the second part of your question—why you were safe here with me last night."

Fargo leaned back and grinned at her. "Maybe you're a crack shot."

"It's not that, Fargo," she said. "Ever since I came to this place, I've felt safe. What I mean is, here I don't worry—these men would never harm me. I've seen it in their faces and noticed it in their manner. No matter how wild they are, they approach me only with respect."

"Strange."

"Yes, but I never question it. I always treated the men who came to my house and to my bed with respect and kindness, no matter how difficult that

93

may have been at times. I can only suppose that this is the way they repay me."

"I hope you're not misjudging these gunslicks, Beverly. They talk about honor among thieves, but I've seen none of it. Cowards, they are, who'd kill a man for a dollar or a bet. And you can never trust them. They're either at your feet or at your throat."

She shrugged. "At any rate, they hide nothing from me—and that, it turns out, is why I decided to help you."

"Oh?"

"As I said last night, I know what you've got in those saddlebags of yours, and that you're looking for a woman called Donna Alvarez. It seems you want to give her half."

"It's what a dying man willed to her, Beverly."

"That's what the word is. And that's why I decided to step in. Any man who's crazy enough to do such a fool thing for a woman has my vote—and my help."

"You mean you might know where I can find this Donna Alvarez?"

Beverly nodded. "Let's say I know where she was heading last time I saw her with that no-account that took her." Beverly pointed out through the window at a range beyond the bluff. "He's on the other side of that range, near a mountain called Widow's Peak. Once you get there, you won't have trouble recognizing it. This Tobias fellow had some crazy notion that there's still gold in an old abandoned silver mine up there. Someone sold the poor son of a bitch a map of some kind." She shook her head at Bart Tobias' gullibility. "Hell! That mine was cleaned out only a year after I settled here. There's nothing left in those drifts but scorpions and the dust of fools."

Fargo took a deep breath. It was a fine lead Beverly had just given him. If he played his cards right, he'd be free of this fool errand and able to shake the trouble that had dogged him ever since Lt. Scott had handed him those heavy sacks of gold dust.

"Thanks, Beverly," Fargo said. "I guess I'll move out this morning and head for those scorpions and dust of fools. Couldn't be much worse than the population of this town—with one exception, of course."

"Exception noted." She smiled. "But don't be so sure I'm not as greedy as the rest, Fargo. About some things, anyway."

She got up from her chair, letting her robe fall open as he did so. With parted lips and lidded eyes, she started across the table toward him. He gazed in some admiration at her large, still-solid breasts, the opulent roundness of her belly, and the lush growth of her pubic triangle.

She kept going until she was pressed against his naked chest and he could feel the heat of her aroused body. With a grin, he thrust his hands between her robe and her ample hips and pulled her close, nuzzling her massive breasts. He felt their incandescence on his cheeks . . . and her hot fingers swiftly unbuttoning his fly.

He stood up to make it easier for her. This time Beverly Smith wasn't going to mind giving it away.

Close to sundown the next day, Fargo topped a rise in sight of Widow's Peak and pulled his weary Ovaro to a halt to let it blow some. Through the draw below him wound a lazy stream and beside it, hunkered down beside his campfire, was a lone prospector, his horse and burro cropping grass on the slope behind him. Pleased at the prospect of company for his supper, Fargo nudged his pinto down the pine-clad slope toward the prospector.

He was almost through the pines when he saw two riders emerge from the timber just below him and, guns blazing, ride hard for the prospector. The old-timer flung around, his own Colt out. Fargo could hear it popping and saw one horse go down, its rider tumbling forward over its neck. But the other rider kept coming, his horse bowling over the prospector, slamming him down into his campfire. As the prospector scrambled free of the fire and jumped to his feet, the rider dismounted and clubbed him back to the ground.

Spurring his pinto out of the pines, Fargo charged down the slope toward the two struggling men. The outlaw heard him coming and spun to face him. As Fargo pounded closer, the outlaw brought up his Colt. But Fargo had already wrapped his reins about his saddle horn and tucked the Sharp's stock into the hollow of his shoulder. He leaned forward slightly, and when his sights caught the gunman's shirtfront, he stroked the trig-

A blinding shaft of light broke in on him. Wincing, he flung his head to one side as he heard a door open and close, followed by the sound of heavy footsteps approaching him. He opened his eyes and turned his head to see the curiously bent figure of the prospector he had attempted to help earlier pausing beside his cot. From his dark complexion and the inky-black color of his hair, which he kept in two long braids, Fargo realized that the prospector, though favoring a white man's dress, had more than a touch of Indian blood in him.

"Awake, are you?" the prospector asked, peering down at Fargo.

Fargo nodded. "Looks like it," he managed.

The prospector smelled of sweaty buckskins and chewing tobacco, but what caught Fargo's attention immediately was the curious way he held his head. It seemed perpetually cocked to one side, almost as if it had been screwed—crookedly and somewhat hastily—down into his shoulders.

"Been wondering when you'd be coming out of it," the prospector said.

"How long have I been here?"

"Close to a week now, counting today."

"My name's Fargo, Skye Fargo. Who're you?"

"I'm called Crooked Elk." His bright-blue eyes snapped mischievously. "I'm sure you can see why."

"The horse I was riding—a pinto. What happened to it?"

"He's getting fat in the pasture below my cabin."

"There were two saddlebags—"

"Filled with gold," Crooked Elk finished, nodding. "Look under the cot if you're wondering where they are."

Fargo took a deep breath. He didn't bother to look. "I'm much obliged to you," he said, deliberately pushing himself to a sitting position. For a moment the tiny room spun about his head before settling back on its foundation. "But right now there's a hole in my stomach. You got anything on the fire."

"Nothing but coffee this early."

"I'll take it." Fargo reached out. "Give me a hand. I'd like to get out of this room. It's too small. I had a bad moment back there when I first came out of it. I thought I was in my coffin, waiting to hear the fresh dirt slapping the top of it."

Crooked Elk chuckled as he helped Fargo off the cot and led him into the kitchen. "I don't blame you," he said. "That's my root cellar. There's no windows, and it ain't all that big, either."

Fargo relieved his bladder outside the cabin, then came back in and slumped gratefully down at the kitchen table. His head was still spinning slightly, but he ignored it as he sipped hot coffee and asked how in the hell he had managed to escape death at the hands of that slack-jawed outlaw who had stood less than five feet away, firing point-blank at him.

Crooked Elk grinned. He had lost a few teeth, but those that remained were a gleaming white. "That no-account was Rap Tinsdale," he explained. "He rode with Moose Bannock. Moose was the one you killed when you rode up. Two lousier shots have

100

never been sent West. Tinsdale's bullet caught your head, all right, but it was only a glancing blow. He never did get a chance to fire a second time. I caught him with my Colt. Him and Moose Bannock've been feeding the buzzards this past week." Crooked Elk grinned. "At first I thought you were dead, too. You must have one hard noggin, Mister."

"Then it looks like I owe you my life."

"More like I owe you mine. If you hadn't ridden up when you did, I'd be a gone beaver."

Fargo shrugged and finished his coffee. "Looks like we make a good team."

Crooked Elk got up and went over to the stove. "You stay easy now," he told Fargo. "I got a muskrat stew brewing. I figure it'll put some flesh back on them bones."

But Fargo was too restless to sit still. He was a man who had just been resurrected from the grave—as far as he was concerned—and he couldn't seem to get enough of the world's smells and sounds, the sheer wonder of it that now swam before his grateful eyes.

He pulled on his boots and, dressed only in his buckskin britches, took a walk outside. He visited his Ovaro first. The horse was grazing on a meadow below the cabin along with Crooked Elk's big gray and the burro. Fargo was pleased to see him, and the handsome pinto was just as pleased in return. The moment Fargo appeared at the edge of the clearing, the pony trotted quickly toward him, bobbing his head up and down in greeting. As Fargo nuzzled the pinto, he wished he'd thought to bring out some sugar with him, but the pinto didn't seem to notice his lapse.

Fargo then took to exploring the high, wild country around Crooked Elk's cabin. It was rugged, almost inaccessible land, the terrain treacherous, the slopes steep. He nearly overdid it and a sudden dizziness forced him to sit down suddenly and rest his back against a small tree until he was steady enough on his feet to make it back to the cabin. Entering it, he was greeted by the stomach-quickening aroma of muskrat stew, bowls of which Crooked Elk was now placing down on the table. The stew was deliciously aromatic and thick with generous chunks of muskrat, beaver tail, potatoes, and a root plant that tasted vaguely like a turnip. The broth was seasoned boldly with wild onions and peppers—the result: a meal solid and nourishing that went a long way to restoring Fargo both mentally and physically.

When the meal was finished and the supper dishes put away, the two men went outside to a bench leaning against the front of the cabin and sat down to watch the sun set. Crooked Elk's cabin was perched on a narrow ridge, and his front yard was a steep slope that plunged toward a heavy stand of pine and aspen about a quarter mile below. By this time the timber was lost in the gathering dusk.

The two men sat in silence for a while, then Fargo asked Crooked Elk about his neck. Or lack of it. He knew it was not the kind of question one man asked another, but he was confident Crooked Elk wouldn't take his curiosity amiss.

"Been wondering when you'd ask about that," Crooked Elk admitted, sending a black dart of chewing tobacco to the ground. "It was a grizzly that done it."

Fargo nodded. "A mean beast when it gets riled."

"Even when he's not riled," Crooked Elk said. He leaned back and began to reminisce. It was clear to Fargo that the man enjoyed talking to a fellow human being, that he in fact relished it. "My mother was a Crow, my pa a trapper from St. Louis who scooted back there soon as he got his first taste of a Rocky Mountain winter. Some missionaries took me in after that and gave me a good dose of English and piety, but I broke loose from them as soon as I got the chance and became a trapper like my pa."

Warming to his topic, Crooked Elk took out a clay pipe and lit up, reminding Fargo that he had some cigars left in one of his saddlebags. Soon the two of them were puffing away contentedly.

"Came back to my camp one bright October afternoon," Crooked Elk resumed, "and found a grizzly in my tent. Tearing up a storm, he was. He'd already ruined a passel of beaver skins, so I wasn't too careful as I went in after him. My rifle misfired. The grizzly swiped at me and took out a chunk of my neck and shoulder. I didn't remember much after that, except him mauling and cuffing at me. He dragged me a ways through the brush before he lost interest." Crooked Elk chuckled. "I think it was my smell made him give up on me."

"You're lucky to be alive."

"That I am. When I got back what little senses I had left, I figured the only way I could stem the bleeding was to tip my head over and lift my shoulder to close the wound. Then I bound up my head and shoulder until the bleeding stopped. Of course, that meant I couldn't straighten my head unless I wanted to rip open the wound again."

Fargo shook his head in wonderment at the man's story. Around many a dim campfire, he had heard a lot of crazy mountain-man stories. This one he believed.

"I was still in bad shape, so I went back to my Mother's people. My mother nursed me through it, but when the wound was finally healed, I found I couldn't straighten my head up. So the Crows gave me my new name, Crooked Elk. I've kept it ever since. I never did like my white name."

"What was that?"

"Charlie Heap."

Fargo chuckled. "I like Crooked Elk better, too."

The two men smoked awhile longer until the mosquitoes took over and they were forced to go back inside.

Despite man-sized portions of muskrat stew and plenty of well-seasoned venison, Fargo's recovery was not as swift as he would have preferred. In the week that followed, he was plagued by intense headaches that erupted whenever he exerted himself. He found riding impossible, and though he chafed under the restrictions, he was forced to keep himself as quiet as possible while Crooked Elk hustled about merrily, hunting and fishing, undoubtedly pleased at the company Fargo provided.

By the end of the second week, Fargo's headaches had grown less frequent and faded markedly in intensity. Soon thereafter his strength began returning, and by the end of the third week, he was almost his old self again. His pinto, meanwhile, had grown fat and sassy and was farting like a banker at his lack of exercise.

Fargo had long since told Crooked Elk about his search for Donna Alvarez and the reason for all that gold he carried in his saddlebags. At the mention of Bart Tobias, Crooked Elk had brightened and told Fargo that he'd seen Tobias working an abandoned mine on the other side of Widow's Peak. He'd also glimpsed a woman helping him, but had been too far away to get a good look at her. He had kept his distance, then ridden on. But he was pretty sure the man was Bart Tobias. Furthermore, he was quite willing to show Fargo the mine Tobias was working, explaining to Fargo that it would give him a chance to check out the mine himself, his own efforts at finding color having proven pretty fruitless until now.

It was after supper. Their bellies were full and they were relaxing on the bench. They were due to pull out the next morning and Crooked Elk had been telling Fargo of the many times he had come close—but not close enough—to a gold strike.

"From what I hear," Fargo commented, "this here country is pretty well played out by now.

You're raking over dead coals. Why not go back north to the Rockies, to where your mother's people are?"

Crooked Elk puffed thoughtfully on his pipe as he thought that over. Finally, he took his pipe out of his mouth and responded. "It's the places the search for gold takes me, I guess. And the poor fools I meet on the way." He looked at Fargo and winked. "Like fellows trying to find women they never saw before. It's better than a circus or a theater show."

Fargo laughed. "How far is that mine you say Tobias is working?"

'A two-day ride at the most.'' Crooked Elk cleared his throat and twisted his upper torso so he could look full upon Fargo. "I been thinking about that gold you're carrying."

"Go on."

"Lugging it around with you makes you a powerful tempting target."

"You got any ideas?"

"Bury it."

"Where?"

"There's a well-hidden cave in the rocks above this cabin. No one would ever find it, unless they knew it was there. You could dig a hole inside it and bury the gold. It'd be safe in there for centuries. No one but me—and now you—even knows that cave's there."

Fargo pulled on his cigar, considering. He sure as hell didn't like hauling all this gold around with him. When he found Donna Alvarez, it would be a simple matter for him to return here with her for the gold.

"Show me the cave," Fargo said.

Crooked Elk chucked. "No hurry. It's not going anywhere. We'll cache the gold in there first thing in the morning, before we pull out."

Fargo nodded. That was good enough for him.

8

The cave was just as Crooked Elk had described it. A huge boulder sat with its backside leaning into the cliff face. In the narrow passage between the boulder and the cliff, a small pine had found a foothold, along with a juniper bush and other brush. Crowding in past the pine and the juniper, Crooked Elk led Fargo to a narrow opening out of sight under a ledge.

On their hands and knees, the two men crawled into the opening, then stood up. Fargo could smell the bats. And the scent—faint but tangible—of the other animals who had, over the centuries, used this cave as their lair. Bear. Puma. Wolf. Coyote. The hair on the back of Fargo's neck raised up slightly.

Crooked Elk lit the torch he had brought. In its flaring light, they both saw a spot along one wall where the soil could be uncovered. Fargo had brought a shovel, and while Crooked Elk held the guttering torch aloft, Fargo dug the hole, dumped the leather pouches into it, then covered them over. As he patted the soil back down with the back of the shovel, he spotted a sizable flat stone off to one side and dragged it over onto the spot beneath which he had just buried his and Donna Alvarez's fortune.

As he stood outside of the cave a moment longer, he looked back at the great boulder, standing like a guardian before the cave's hidden entrance. "I hope the next time I crawl into that cave," he told Crooked Elk, "I don't meet something wild and frightened."

Crooked Elk shook his head. "You won't. The smell of man is too strong in there now."

They moved off.

Two days later, close on to dusk, they topped a rock-strewn ridge and peered down at the abandoned mine site where Crooked Elk had last seen Bart Tobias.

By the look of things, Bart Tobias was still there. A mean, windowless shack constructed out of tar paper and raw lumber sat on a rise about a hundred yards back of the mine entrance, and from old beams and weathered siding Bart Tobias had fashioned a crude corral behind a building large enough to use as a barn. A burro was at the far end, down on its knees, in a shaded portion just behind the barn.

They urged their mounts down the shale-littered slope, approaching the mine from the north. The late sun slanted into their eyes as they peered about at the piles of tailings and the assorted tools and equipment left by the miners when it came time to abandon the diggings. Rusted ore cars sat crookedly in the earth, half-filled with sand, some with juniper and scrub pine growing in them. The high trestles that once carried the rails for the ore cars were crumbling and hanging above them was a tangle of beams and cross ties, like some strange, leafless tree that had sprung from the barren, denuded slopes.

The roof of the building over the mine shaft had fallen in, and peering up at it, Fargo realized how difficult gaining entrance to the mine shaft now must be. He wondered then at the foolhardiness of a man who, in his desperate search for gold, would brave such a tangle of rotted beams and treacherous, unsecured shafts.

Once again, it seemed, Fargo was reminded of what men would do for gold.

"Something's wrong," Crooked Elk said, reining in his mount and peering closely at the shack.

Fargo reined in also. He didn't know what had disturbed Crooked Elk, but Fargo himself had begun to notice how dark the shack was. Dusk had fallen. If there were people inside, a light would be showing through a crack somewhere and some smoke would be coming from the stovepipe chimney poking out of the side.

"People leave a smell," Crooked Elk said. "The smell of wood burning, food cooking, fresh horse manure. The smell here is very little."

Crooked Elk nudged his horse forward again, and a moment later they dismounted in front of the shack and entered. Dirty dishes were standing in the wooden bucket, crumbs still loose on the plates. A chair was overturned, and the bed in one corner looked as if someone had just got up from it. The fire in the potbellied stove was out, but peering into the belly, Fargo saw one or two tiny red coals gleaming at him from a bed of white ashes.

"Breakfast fire's still alive," Fargo said. "Barely."

"I think there's been trouble here," Crooked Elk said.

"I think so, too," Fargo said, frowning. "Maybe we better check out the mine—and fast."

"I'll look for lanterns," Crooked Elk said. "Get some digging tools."

Not long after, with Crooked Elk carrying two lighted lanterns and Fargo a pickax and shovel, they hurried from the shack toward the mine-shaft entrance. They were within a couple of hundred yards of a recently constructed wooden ladder that led up to the entrance when a rifle shot came at them from somewhere on the slope above. Both men flung themselves into a hollow alongside the ladder. Fargo heard one of the lanterns shatter, Crooked Elk's curse coming soon after.

"Maybe you better put out that lantern," Fargo told him.

But before Crooked Elk could reach it, another shot exploded the lantern, sending flaming shards of glass over both men.

Fargo beat out one shard that landed on his leg and glanced up the slope. "Son of a bitch," he said. "That bastard's one helluva marksman. He's after our lanterns, and it only took him two shots."

"It'll be dark soon," Crooked Elk said. "Then we'll get him."

But when night came, they found themselves still pinned in the hollow. Whoever it was up there had cat's eyes, and anytime they made a move for the ladder or tried to go back to the cabin, the ground around them began jumping with bullets. By this time, they realized that whoever it was had one of those new Spencer repeaters. When they kept real still, they could hear him cranking each new shell into its magazine.

The moon came up, and the slope above them became a little clearer as did the collapsed, ruined buildings from which they had decided the rifle fire was coming. When they finally made a run for the ladder, the rifleman coolly picked away at the rungs above them, shattering them. They gave it up, and took cover under a wooden sluice, realizing they were going to have to wait it out until daylight—or until the marksman above them grew tired of his game.

A little after midnight they heard the faint thunder of a horse's hooves. Sitting bolt upright, Crooked Elk listened, then turned to Fargo. "He's gone now, I think."

Fargo poked his head out from under the sluice and moved toward the ladder, keeping his head low. He started climbing and reached as far as the shattered rungs before calling down to Crooked Elk, "You're right. He's gone. But we won't be able to get up this way—not now."

"I say we go back to the cabin and wait until daylight."

"Good idea," Fargo agreed.

About nine o'clock the next day they found the drift Bart Tobias was working.

The evidence was visible everywhere. A wheelbarrow loaded with freshly mined ore. Picks. Shovels. Drills. Blasting powder. Coils of Bickford fuses. Everything but Tobias himself—or Donna Alvarez. Holding their lanterns high and moving warily along the drift, the two men called out repeatedly.

It was Fargo who spotted the rope tied to a beam. It was taut and led down into a vertical shaft. On his hands and knees, Fargo peered over the edge. He could see nothing but blackness, and felt a cold, clammy wind fanning his face. The shaft appeared to go down forever.

"Give me some light," Fargo said.

Behind him, Crooked Elk reached over with his lantern, sending enough light down the tunnel to enable Fargo's eyes to follow the rope and see the man at the end of it—as still as death.

Beside Fargo, Crooked Elk grunted. The two men hauled up the body. Fargo had never seen Bart Tobias, but Crooked Elk had, even if from a distance, and he identified the man without hesitation. Tobias hadn't died by hanging; the rope was around his waist. It was the kitchen knife in his back that had killed him.

"The way I see it," Fargo said, stepping away from the body, "he was stabbed first. Then whoever did it tied the rope around his waist and pushed him over."

"Why do that?"

"I was thinking that myself. Whoever killed him could have just stabbed him and pushed him over, and no one would have been the wiser. What I think is that Tobias was still alive when he was pushed over. Whoever did it wanted him to twist awhile down in that shaft—think about it a bit, maybe scream himself hoarse. Look at those eyes. They're still wide with terror."

Crooked Elk nodded. "I think maybe you're right."

"The thing is, where's the girl . . . Donna?"

"Don't you know, Fargo?"

Fargo looked back at the body of Bart Tobias, the man who had beaten, then taken Donna Alvarez from Tularosa after lying about all the gold he had stashed away. Yes, of course he knew where Donna Alvarez was. She was that rifleman the night before, and a little after midnight it was she they had heard galloping away.

Donna had killed Bart Tobias and then fired on them to keep them from entering the mine and finding Tobias too soon, before he had time to die. As they approached the mine last night, Tobias had probably still been twisting on the end of the rope, screaming. Once they entered the mine, they would have heard him. Donna had kept them out with some very fancy shooting.

"That Donna Alvarez, she's one fine shot," Crooked Elk said, shaking his head in admiration.

"Yes," Fargo said. He looked back at the dead man. She was also, he realized, one fine cold-blooded killer.

They found the tracks left by the horse they assumed Donna Alvarez was riding. She was heading northwest, it appeared. The closest town in that direction was Twin Butte, a two-day ride. Neither man knew what Donna Alvarez looked like, but if she was in Twin Butte, they figured they couldn't go far wrong if they looked for a woman who carried a Spencer repeating rifle and knew how to use it.

They started for Twin Butte that afternoon and camped in the mountains that night. After they ate, Fargo took out a cigar and settled down on a log to watch the campfire die out. Crooked Elk fished in his saddlebag for his clay pipe, and for a while the two men smoked in silence.

It was Fargo who spoke up finally. "She certainly hated Tobias."

Crooked Elk removed the pipe from his mouth and spat into the fire. "You're wondering if she's worth chasing all over hell and beyond to give her that share of the gold."

Fargo nodded. That was it all right.

"Well, you got to remember," Crooked Elk said.

"A woman's got a right to kill if she's been wronged—just like a man has."

Fargo nodded, feeling somewhat better.

"Of course, that's not the whole of it. And I figure you know that, too," Crooked Elk continued.

Fargo looked at Crooked Elk. "You mean gold?"

Crooked Elk put the pipe back in his mouth and puffed awhile before responding. "I looked over some of that ore Tobias had piled in one of his wheelbarrows. Looks to me like he'd come on some color, sure enough. I figure this woman waited her chance, killed him, and took the best of the gold ore with her. That way, she not only gets even, she gets rich."

Fargo took a deep drag on his cigar. He too had seen that gold trace on the ore, and though he hated to admit it, what Crooked Elk said made damn good sense.

"If we're right," Crooked Elk said, "she's going to be real hard to track down. She got a good look at us, and she'll have to figure we found Tobias and know she's the one killed him. So if she sees us coming, she just might hightail it."

"She'll be a fool if she does," Fargo said. "She'll miss out on her share of that gold I stashed."

"You still want her to have it?"

"It's not what I want or don't want. I made a promise," Fargo reminded him.

Crooked Elk said nothing. He just leaned back and puffed on his clay pipe. After a while, he finished his smoke, rapped the bowl of his pipe against a boulder, then went over to his bedroll and curled up. Fargo stayed on the log until the fire was little more than winking embers in the night's cool darkness. Then he got up and went over to his own bedroll.

He went to sleep wondering if he wasn't seven kinds of a fool.

Though still a small town, surrounded by sheer, snow-capped peaks, Twin Butte considered itself a growing metropolis, a town with a future. There was talk of a railroad, a link that would tie the town into the long-discussed cross-country rail network destined to link the East Coast to the West Coast. Of course, it looked like it was going to have to wait until that blamed nuisance of a war back East sputtered out, but that wouldn't be long—not if you listened to the barbers or to the merchants in the saloons and restaurants.

Fargo and Crooked Elk found rooms at the Mountain Home, a hotel across from the Wells Fargo office, then went in search of a barbershop that also had hot tubs in the rear. After that, they found a saloon not far from the hotel that was the biggest and flashiest either had frequented in a long, long time.

Crooked Elk, with his twisted neck and long, black, braided hair, wasn't a man one could ignore, and it wasn't long after Fargo and he had made themselves comfortable that two men, primed to the gills on bravo juice, journeyed over to their table to introduce themselves.

With a barely perceptible nod passing between

them, Fargo and Crooked Elk each sized up their own man. Fargo's was a huge, barrel-chested fellow with a black beard and a head as bald and shiny as a brass cuspidor. His nose was a wreck, and he no longer had all his teeth—a brawler by profession, judging from the marks on him.

"Go get 'em, Baldy," someone at the bar shouted.

Grinning, Baldy pulled up in front of the table and planted himself firmly, while his companion—a rangy redhead so hard-muscled he looked as if he had been fashioned from coils of rope—stood alertly to one side, arms folded, waiting.

It was Baldy who spoke up first. "What in the hell are you doing bringing a half-breed in here, mister?"

"What the hell does it look like?"

"Get out. Both of you. You're not welcome!"

"And if that crooked freak show sitting beside you's not out of town by nightfall," added the redhead, "you'll both end up swinging under a full moon."

"That the law in this town?" Fargo asked him.

"It's our law."

"Since when?"

"Since you two walked in here and stank up the place," Baldy said.

"Well," Fargo drawled, reaching for the neck of his whiskey bottle, "if you two think you can make it stick go ahead."

That was the signal. The four men lunged at one another, crunching together like bull elks at mating season. The sound of bottles crashing on skulls and the grunts of their sudden exertions filled the saloon. At once the patrons moved aside, forming a rough ring around the combatants. Evidently, this wasn't an uncommon occurrence.

Fargo was being pressed hard. Very hard. He had broken his whiskey bottle over Baldy's head, but it had little discernible effect on the man. Grinning, Baldy had just put his head down and bore in on Fargo, his arms like pistons as they chopped solidly at Fargo's head and body. Soon Fargo's ribs were sore and his forearms aching from warding off Baldy's sledging blows.

But Fargo stood his ground, flailing away at Baldy with considerable effect, landing solid punches about the man's neck and face and quickly drawing blood from a cut under his right eye. Yet this did not faze Baldy at all, and Fargo realized he was in a battle with an experienced brawler, one whose sole recreation was to take on any newcomers who showed up in this saloon. Behind Baldy's weaving, bobbing head, Fargo glimpsed the barkeep almost casually placing a long wooden shield up against the bar mirror, then removing the bottles from the shelves, while two of his aproned assistants pulled some of the tables and chairs off the floor and hauled the chandeliers up out of harm's way.

A sudden punch caught Fargo on his nose. Lights exploded deep inside his head. Blinking frantically to clear his vison, he reeled back, a warm freshet of blood pouring down across his upper lip and into his mouth. His eyes alight, Baldy followed Fargo relentlessly and caught him with a powerful round-house punch on the right ear, ringing his bell soundly. Fargo felt his knees turning to oatmeal, but managed to fling up his guard as Baldy quickly moved in. So anxious was Baldy to finish Fargo off that he got careless and let loose with a roundhouse right that only nicked Fargo's chin, while it left him wide open.

Fargo stepped forward and caught Baldy flush on his chin, staggering him, then followed it up with two quick jabs, each quick punch snapping Baldy's head back. Baldy slowed up, blinked, and tried to pull back. But Fargo crowded him against the wall and began working him over with vicious, methodical precision.

By now Fargo had his second wind and was beginning to enjoy himself, fighting with an icy calculation that seemed to give him a second or two of anticipation for every punch Baldy let fly. With calm, metronomic blows, he began cutting the brawler's face apart, until his black beard was red with blood. Watching Baldy's eyes, Fargo saw them begin to lose their sharp, angry glint.

But when he stepped back to measure one final, devastating blow, Baldy saw it coming and lunged forward. He grappled Fargo around the waist with his treelike arms and dragged him to the floor. Fargo felt a chair crunch into kindling under him, and then the two men were rolling over and over in the sawdust, punching, biting, gouging. It was as if Baldy had regained his strength the moment he touched the floor. He was wrestling now as much as punching, and suddenly Baldy's full weight crunched down onto Fargo, crushing him beneath his considerable bulk. Grabbing Fargo's arm, he flung the Trailsman over onto his face and began twisting his arm up behind his back in what appeared to be a deliberate attempt to rip Fargo's arm out of its socket.

With a desperate, furious burst, Fargo managed to fling himself over, dislodging Baldy and freeing his right arm. Baldy rocked back on his heels, cuffed Fargo, then flung an awkward punch at him. Skye grabbed the man's hand with both of his, then jumped to his feet, twisting the brawler's hand around sharply. With a painful grunt, Baldy gave in quickly, turning his back on Fargo to relieve the pressure.

Fargo placed his foot in the small of the brawler's back and pushed hard, at the same time yanking back his hand with a quick, vicious snap. A sharp, cracking sound filled the shocked saloon, and Fargo released his grip so that he didn't tear Baldy's hand completely off his arm. His face twisted in agony, Baldy sank to his knees, cradling his shattered, useless right wrist. His face was a pasty white as he looked down and saw that the only thing holding his hand to his right arm was a purplish mass of torn flesh.

Fargo glanced over in time to see Crooked Elk spin around a couple of times with the redhead over his head, then hurl him through the saloon's window. Crashing through it, the redhead came down on the hitch rack outside, snapping it with a report that sounded like a gunshot. Turning his attention back to Baldy, Fargo advanced on him. The brawler was barely conscious by this time, so agonizing was the pain in his ruined wrist. And it would get a whole lot worse, Fargo realized, before it got any better. More than likely, his hand would have to be amputated.

The brawler looked up at Fargo, his eyes wide in shock and horror. "You broke it off," he quavered. "Clean off!"

"So I did," Fargo told him.

"I'm a cripple."

"You already were," Fargo told him. "Now get out of town before nightfall. You and your sidekick. Or the next thing you lose will be the use of your fool neck."

The big man scrambled to his feet and lurched from the saloon.

Fargo looked around at the astonished, staring patrons. "What's wrong?" he asked them. "Cheer up. I'm buying."

With a whoop, the patrons stampeded toward the bar.

9

It soon turned out that Fargo and Crooked Elk had done the saloon—and the town—a service. After Fargo paid for the round, the saloon's patrons allowed neither Fargo nor Crooked Elk to pay for another drink. And as the news spread throughout Twin Butte that Baldy and his vicious sidekick had finally been routed, the two men became heroes, welcome everywhere—celebrities.

The reason was soon made obvious to the two men: with Baldy and his companion on the loose, the reputation of the town had begun to suffer, and any chances of attracting that railhead hub the town's boosters were praying for was about to go a-glimmering.

Unfortunately, this notoriety was the last thing Fargo wanted. He had hoped to be able to drift unnoticed into Twin Butte, make his inquiries concerning Donna Alvarez as quietly as possible, then move on if he had no luck in tracing her. Such a course of action was now impossible.

The first thing they had done when they rode into Twin Butte was to inquire at the livery stable about a woman riding in alone with a Spencer rifle as part of her gear. No such woman had used the livery, they were informed. Still, Fargo reasoned, that didn't mean Donna Alvarez wasn't in Twin Butte. If she *had* reached the town before them, after all this fuss, she'd most certainly have had Fargo and Crooked Elk pointed out to her. If so, there was a chance she would recognize them as the two men she had kept from entering the mine. This would prompt her either to keep herself hidden or to slip out of town at the first opportunity.

Accordingly, Fargo stationed Crooked Elk on the hotel's veranda within sight of the livery stable and the Wells Fargo Express office. He wanted the Indian to monitor all arrivals and departures. Crooked Elk allowed as how that didn't appear to be a hopelessly difficult task, took out his clay pipe, and settled into a wicker chair.

Fargo then visited the express office to ask if a woman had come in with recently mined gold dust or nuggets to be assayed or shipped out. No woman had, Fargo was assured. When he asked the officers of the local bank if a woman had tried to exchange gold ore for bank notes, he got the same result. After that, Fargo went to all the town's clothing stores and dress shops, inquiring as unobtrusively as possible about a woman, new in town, who might be shopping somewhat extravagantly.

He got nowhere. If Donna Alvarez was in Twin Butte, she was sure as hell keeping out of sight. On the other hand, there was always the chance he'd passed her a dozen times on the street and not known it, since he had never seen her himself. She was of Spanish descent. That much he knew from Michelle's description of her. Her hair was dark and her eyes would be also. Fargo imagined her to be tall, but she might very well be short. Whatever her height, she was pretty enough and had a figure enticing enough to attract a man with the hungers of a Bart Tobias.

But by the end of the week, after finding no trace of Donna Alvarez, Fargo was close to deciding that there was little sense in continuing much longer in this fruitless quest.

Saturday afternoon the two men found themselves catching the slanting rays of the sun on the hotel veranda, watching the traffic that rattled past the hotel. They were also trying not to notice the heavy stench of horse manure and fresh horse piss. It had been a particularly hot day, with not a single cloud in the sky. And the welcome chill of evening was still some hours away.

A handsome woman under a light-green, lacy parasol paused in front of the veranda at sight of the two men, turned, and mounted the steps. As she walked across the veranda toward them, she lowered her parasol and Fargo found himself looking into two lovely, smoky-brown eyes. Her boldness and the way she carried herself left no doubt of her profession, but Fargo and Crooked Elk got quickly to their feet, doffing their hats politely.

"Good afternoon, gentlemen," the woman said. "Would you think me too bold if I presumed to join you?"

"Not at all," said Fargo, grabbing a wicker chair and holding it for her.

Hatless, she wore her auburn hair in thick curls that rested lightly on her broad shoulders. Her face was angular, but not hard, with high cheekbones, a firm, square jaw, and lips full and passionate, with just a touch of lipstick. She was wearing a bottle-green outfit, all ruffles and lace, so snug on her it looked as if she'd had to pour herself into it. Flowing up from her tiny waist was a bountiful pair of beauties. Her daring, lace-fringed neckline was cut low, and as Fargo bent over her to adjust her chair, he didn't miss the opportunity she gave him to glimpse the light sprinkling of freckles across her bosom and the magnificent cleft into which he almost fell. As she settled back in her chair, she crossed her legs, revealing her black, stockinged ankles and high button shoes.

She introduced herself as Mattie Holbrook and without hesitation gave the address of the parlor house she kept on Mountain Street.

"My girls are clean, sir," she said proudly, "and know how to treat a man. They are a merry band, as lewd as monkeys, but they laugh easily and make a man glad he came to visit. But I must say we've all been disappointed this past week, wondering why you haven't visited us. It'd be a shame if you left Twin Butte without allowing us to thank you personally."

"Thank us?" Fargo repeated.

She laughed. "But of course! Do you have any idea what a tribulation those two men you ran out of town had been for me and my girls? Because of them, some of my best girls had run off—to far less hospitable towns, I assure you—simply because they could no longer tolerate those two animals."

Fargo smiled. He didn't find it difficult to imagine the kind of trouble those two could generate in a parlor house. No wonder Mattie had made so bold as to introduce herself to them.

"Well, then," he said, "in that case, you can count on a visit from me soon. If there's one thing I appreciate, it is the heartfelt gratitude of a woman."

"And that you shall have. I promise you."

"How about tonight?"

She brightened. "We'd be delighted."

"There's just one thing."

"Name it."

"You've been talking to me all this time. Crooked Elk goes where I go. I just thought I ought to mention it."

She glanced quickly at Crooked Elk. "Please forgive me," she told him. "I didn't mean to exclude you in this conversation. Of course you are most welcome—indeed, Crooked Elk, I would be pleased to thank you myself, personally."

Crooked Elk smiled, leaned forward, and patted the madam lightly on her knee. "I'll hold you to that, Mattie," he told her with a grin.

She laughed, a genuine, deep laugh that warmed them both; then she got to her feet. "Thank you, gentlemen, for your courtesy in receiving me so openly. You will not regret it, I promise you. Until this evening, then."

The two men watched Mattie stride off, her parasol twirling. It was Crooked Elk who spoke up first, his voice hushed, "She's a real pippin, that one. It's been a long time for me. I sure as hell hope I still got what it takes."

"Don't worry," Fargo told him. "I got the impression she'll know how to take care of that."

Crooked Elk leaned back in his chair and nodded, a wide grin on his face. "I got that same impression."

An hour or so later, they were on the way to what had become their favorite restaurant when Fargo pulled up suddenly. Glancing down a side alley, he'd spotted Doc Gurney ducking into one of the cheaper saloons. The physician had looked even more threadbare and disreputable than he had in Pine Top. At once Fargo was wary. If Doc Gurney was in Twin Butte, there was a damn good chance that Slats Tarnell was with him.

"You see a ghost or something?" Crooked Elk asked, pulling up also.

"Not a ghost—worse. You go on ahead. Order me a steak. I won't be long."

With a shrug, Crooked Elk continued on to the restaurant, leaving Fargo to duck down the alley and into the saloon. The place was noisy and packed solid, with heavy layers of coiling smoke reaching clear to the ceiling. Pushing his way through the crush, Fargo saw the doc squeezed into a chair beside a table in the rear. He had purchased a cheap bottle of whiskey and was busy pouring himself a drink, his hand shaking noticeably. As Fargo pushed through the sweaty bodies toward his table, the doc took hold of the shot glass with both hands and carefully lifted it to his mouth and began sipping it as if he were terrified he might lose a drop. He was obviously in a bad way. For the first time in his life, Fargo knew what "Physician Heal Thyself" meant.

Slapping the glass back down on the table, the doc was reaching for the bottle when Fargo dragged over a chair and joined him at the table. With a cold smile, Fargo snatched up the whiskey bottle and set it down beyond his reach.

"What the hell are you doing?" the man bleated pitiably. "That's my bottle."

"Where's Slats Tarnell?"

"How the hell should I know?"

"Are you telling me he's not in Twin Butte with you?"

"Goddammit, I don't have to answer no questions from you. Now give me that bottle."

"You look all done in, Doc," Fargo said. "And the way you were hanging on to that glass, it's been a long time since you had the price of a drink. What's Slats doing? Keeping you on a tight rein?"

The whites of Doc Gurney's eyes were yellow, his sunken face unshaven, and he smelled bad. He looked from Fargo to the bottle, then back to Fargo. Licking his parched lips, he said, "If I tell you, will you let me have that bottle back?"

Fargo took hold of the bottle. "Sure."

"He was with me, but he's gone now. I don't know where he is. He made me stay with him until he was well enough to ride."

"When was this?"

"Last week."

"You're lying. Who gave you the money for this bottle?"

Doc Gurney looked as if he were going to cry. "I . . . took a slug out of a guy's ass. He just paid me."

"I don't believe you."

"All right! All right! Tarnell gave me the money. But I don't know where he is now! I swear! He says he's better now and doesn't need me around. He kicked me out, I tell you."

Fargo had no difficulty at all in believing that Tarnell had kicked out the doctor. That the doc didn't know where Tarnell was now, however, he found impossible to believe. But short of beating the doc up in plain sight of fifty or more saloon patrons, there was little more he could reasonably hope to find out from him.

Fargo pushed the bottle across the table to the little man and stood up. "Drink up, Doc. But I got some advice before I go."

With shaking hands, Gurney grabbed the bottle and began to fill his shot glass. His voice quavering, he asked , "Advice? What advice you got?"

"A bullet's a whole lot cleaner and a helluva lot quicker than that bottle."

The doctor stared up at him for a moment, blinking miserably, then went back to filling up his shot glass, his hand still shaking. Fargo turned his back on the man and pushed his way through the crush of loud, whiskey-besotted patrons to the alley outside.

The smell of pure horse manure coming from a nearby livery stable was almost refreshing.

Mattie's girls were just as eager to please as she'd promised Fargo and Crooked Elk they would be. In expectation of their visit, she had closed her parlor house to other guests. As a result, it was late in the evening before either of them were released from the horny clutches of their pretty little tormentors, all of whom had obviously been given the delightful task of warming up their two honored guests.

At midnight—the witching hour—Mattie herself, wearing a filmy pink nightdress that left nothing to the imagination, appeared at the head of the stairs. With a single crick of her forefinger she brought the eager Crooked Elk up the stairs to her side. With a wave to the rest of her girls, Mattie drew Crooked Elk after her as she led the way to her room. By that time there was no doubt in Fargo's mind—or Crooked Elk's either—that he was ready and able to please his hostess. The bulge in his crotch had long since became a highly visible object of merriment for the delightful swarm of temptresses who had been deviling him all night.

Fargo had had his eye on a long-legged Spanish beauty from the very beginning of the night's revels. She had returned his interest, but from a calculated distance, delighting in teasing him with occasional lewd grabs at his crotch or lingering kisses that inflamed his vitals. Now, as he made his choice unmistakable and allowed her to lead him up the stairs, the other girls ran lightly ahead of them, carrying on like a troop of lewd imps, revealing breasts, buns, muffs, in a coarse and delightful display of good humor.

As Mattie had promised, her girls knew how to please a man.

The girl had told Fargo her name was Teresa, but as soon as the door closed behind them and she flung off her gown to stand naked before Fargo, he smiled. "I've been looking a long time for you, Donna."

"Was it worth the wait, Skye?"

He looked her over, his groin twitching. She was a column of dusky flesh, with long thighs tapering up from her trim calves to a lush black pubic patch that covered the lower portion of her gently swelling belly. Her mature, powerful hips arced dramatically into the curve of her narrow waist, and above them her full breasts swelled, their rosettes already pebbling and their tips beginning to pucker and thrust outward.

"Yes," he said. "It was worth the wait."

Smiling, she undid his belt and slipped his buckskins down over his narrow hips, then undid his shirt. He kicked off his boots and socks and she led him over to the bed. She sat him down, then washed him off with warm, caressing hands. Finished, she stood before him.

"I am glad it was worth the wait," she said, pushing him back onto the bed and climbing swiftly up onto him, rubbing her muff eagerly against his straining erection.

Fargo decided he would talk of Walt Tennyson's legacy to her later; at the moment all he wanted to do was impale her with his aching shaft. He rolled her over quickly and with his big hands lifted her buns and slid her under him, then came down, hard. She spread her legs swiftly, deftly, arching up as she did so, and he entered her smoothly, plunging all the way to the bottom. Her gasp became a cry as she tightened around his erection and flung her arms about his neck to squeeze him closer to her. He felt her body go taut as he began his powerful thrusting, going deeper with each massive stroke.

"Ah, yes!" Donna whispered hoarsely, her arms still tight around his neck, her breath on his ear. "This too I have waited a long time for. I know when I see you, it would be like this."

Fargo kept right on stroking, building steadily. His lips found hers. Her mouth yawned wide, hungrily, and his darting tongue met hers in a lascivious embrace. He kept up his stroking, meanwhile, driving still deeper, feeling her shudder with each powerful thrust. Her hands grabbed at the back of his head now, holding him in the kiss as Fargo continued thrusting into her, feeling the sobs surging deep in her throat.

Moments passed and he didn't slow the quick tempo of his thrusting until she writhed under him again, and the sobs trapped in her throat brought her breasts pressing against the hard muscles of his chest. He was reaching for his own orgasm now, and drove into her with long, hard strokes. Then, when he felt Donna's quivering become a series of quick, convulsive jerks, he let go and fell forward onto her, still keeping her lips trapped with his until the laxness of her muscles told him that the time of her need to scream had passed. He took his lips away and let her drain her lungs of the breath trapped within them.

"My God!" she gasped. "You do not make love, Skye. You fuck."

"That was a pretty long time coming for me," Fargo said by way of apology. "Maybe too long."

"Do not apologize. Such a need I understand. I am human, too, Skye. Later tonight, we will experiment with other ways. Maybe I show you a few tricks, eh?"

"Sure thing, Donna—if you think you haven't wrung me out yet."

"Such a man as you does not get wrung out so easy, I think."

He shrugged and pushed himself back against the headboard, his head resting against a pillow. Donna moved up beside him and rested her head on his chest, her fingers tracing idly the area around his hips. He felt himself begin to stir to life, but ignored it.

"From what I gather," he said, "you knew I was looking for you."

"Yes."

"And you knew I was in Twin Butte?"

"But of course, Skye. You and Crooked Elk are most famous in this town for what you do to those terrible men."

"Then why didn't you come forward?"

"At first I not know why you want me. I not believe what some say. Why would a man chase a woman to give her gold? And then when I see you, I remember the mine—and what I had to do then to keep you away. So I think that is why you chase me."

"So that was you, wasn't it—behind that Spencer rifle, I mean."

She lifted her head off his chest and looked at him, her eyes wide with concern. "Now you are angry with Donna?"

He shook his head. "I figure Tobias got what was coming to him. From what I hear, he wasn't worth much."

"He lie to me. Then he make me his slave. And he beat me. I will show you my back. The stripes, they have not yet healed."

"I believe you. So you killed him."

Her eyes glittered in the darkened room. "I kill him slow, so he know he is going to die. He hang in the darkness of that shaft and wait for death to come. For a long while," she said with some satisfaction, "he pleaded with me, begged me. He died screaming."

"And you didn't want us to stop that."

"No. Donna Alvarez wait long for this revenge. If you save him, you cheat me of what I plan for long time."

Fargo didn't shudder, but he felt a coldness close about his heart at this evidence of Donna Alvarez' implacable nature. She had been wronged and beaten, treated badly, it was true. Yet, there was something so frighteningly primitive in Donna's response that it gave him pause.

"There's some Indian blood in you, Donna."

"And you too, Skye," she said, snuggling closer. "I could tell the moment I see you."

He said nothing, feeling the warmth of her, his hunger for her building again within him. She'd been right. A man like him didn't get wrung out easily.

"Is it true, Skye?"

"Is what true?"

"That you have gold for me?"

"It's true."

"Where is it?"

"I don't have it with me. I hid it for safekeeping."

"Where?"

"Back near Crooked Elk's cabin. Don't worry. It's safe enough."

"And when will you bring it to me?"

"I'll send Crooked Elk back for it tomorrow."

She said nothing for a moment, then in a soft, hushed voice, she asked, "And how much gold will you have for me?"

"Your share's a couple of thousand."

He heard her sharp intake of breath, then she asked, "My share? What do you mean?"

"You remember a fellow named Walt Tennyson?"

"I remember. He was fine man. I love him, I think . . . for a little while, anyway. He need money, so I give him some. He have dream of making much money by selling horse to soldiers, I think. Then he left and I never see him again."

"He died. But before he did, he made me promise to give you his share of what we got when we sold the horses."

"Ah! I see!" She lifted her head again to gaze on him in wonder. "And so you keep your vow."

"It was a blood oath. Walt was dying. And the only one he was thinking about was you."

"It is . . . sad," she said, her voice small. "How did he die?"

"Apaches wounded him, paralyzed him from the waist down. I shot him."

She was astonished. "You shot him?"

"So the Apaches wouldn't get him."

She was silent for a long while, then she pulled herself closer to him, hugging him suddenly. "You are very strong man," she said. "You have big heart. I think now maybe I want to make love to you again."

He wasn't quite ready yet, he thought. He still had questions he wanted to ask. But when Donna Alvarez' lips moved down to his groin, then past it, he found himself caught up once more in the savage frenzy of their coupling.

10

The next day Fargo returned to the neighborhood where he had caught sight of Doc Gurney the evening before. He stationed himself on a porch in front of a general store and kept his eye on the alley down which Gurney had ducked. About four o'clock in the afternoon Fargo spotted Gurney, looking reasonably sober, approaching.

Fargo left the porch in a single stride and overtook Doc Gurney before he could turn down the alley. Grabbing him by the arm, he spun the little man around. "Hi, Doc."

"Leave me be, Fargo!"

"You're sober now. Cold sober, looks like. I'd like to have a talk with you."

Pulling himself free of Fargo, Doc Gurney straightened himself up and stared with desperate defiance at Fargo. "Go ahead, then. Talk."

"Not here. Your place."

"You have no authority over me!"

Fargo chuckled and grabbed the scrawny man's arm, just above his elbow. Squeezing the man's thin arm, he said, "Here's my authority."

"But . . ." Gurney protested, glancing down the alley at the saloon entrance. "I need a drink."

"And you'll get one—soon as we have our little chat. Where're you staying?"

Doc Gurney moistened his dry lips. "The Border Lands Hotel. In the back of the feed mill. But why do we have to go that far?"

"Never mind why. Move it."

With great reluctance Doc Gurney allowed Fargo to accompany him to his hotel. The building was completely rundown. Fargo had no trouble imagining the cockroaches on the walls and the seam squirrels in the bedding that must have kept the doc's night eventful—if he wasn't too drunk to notice.

There was no one at the front desk to challenge them as Fargo followed an increasingly nervous Doc Gurney up the stairs to his room. With a shaking hand, the doc let Fargo into his room, then followed in after him.

The single bed was narrow; the dresser was missing a drawer; and the window shade was torn and hung askew against the dirty windowpanes. Fargo was disappointed. His first quick glance at the dim, narrow room told him that the doctor was alone. There was no sign whatsoever of a companion. At least, not in this tiny, airless room. He turned to the doc. "All right. Now take me to Tarnell's room."

Doc Gurney hesitated and was about to deny that Tarnell had a room at the hotel, when Fargo spun him roughly around and told him to move it. With a fatalistic shrug, the doctor led Fargo down the hallway to another room. He knocked once on the door and pushed it open.

Drawing his Colt, Fargo followed Doc Gurney into the room. It was empty and absent of all signs of occupancy. The drawers in the dresser were all pulled out and empty, evidence that the room's occupant had packed in a hurry. Watching the doctor, Fargo saw the way the little man's shoulders sagged in relief.

"When did he leave?" Fargo asked.

Doc Gurney shrugged.

"You fixed him up good and proper, did you?"

The doctor straightened and with some pride said, "He's as good as new, with full use of his right arm and shoulder."

"So you do all that for Tarnell, and he runs out on you."

Doc Gurney smiled, but it was more like a silent snarl. "Gratitude," he said, "is not a human trait. A dog won't bite the hand of a man who feeds him. This, I find, is the chief difference between men and dogs."

Fargo looked carefully at the grim little sawbones. He had the nagging feeling he was missing something, but he couldn't come up with what it was. He dropped his Colt back into his holster. "See you, Doc."

"Yes," the man said, his voice quavering slightly with indignation. "I'm sure you will."

It was past midnight, and Fargo and Crooked Elk were standing in the darkness behind the livery stable. Crooked Elk had saddled his mount without the hostler's knowledge. Fargo had seen to that by strolling into the livery earlier to check on his Ovaro and then passing a bottle to the old-timer who worked nights.

"I'll be back in less than a week," Crooked Elk promised Fargo as he stepped up into his saddle. "You keep them girls happy while I'm gone."

Fargo moved back to peer up at his friend. He still felt uneasy, but he had promised Donna they would bring her the gold—and for his part, Fargo was anxious to be rid of it. It was more a curse than a blessing.

"Watch your ass," Fargo told him.

"That I will," said Crooked Elk, and with a quick wave he cut down the alley. In a moment horse and rider had disappeared into the darkness.

Fargo walked back through the alley, then headed across the street to his hotel. His plan was to stay in full view until Crooked Elk returned with the gold, hoping in the meantime to draw out Slats Tarnell and finish him off once and for all. He was certain that Tarnell was still in town, waiting his chance. There was no way Tarnell was going to give up on that gold—or on his desire to even the score with Fargo.

Earlier that day, Fargo had made a conspicuous appearance at the town's largest bank, a bulging pair of saddlebags slung over his shoulder. Once in the bank, he had asked to see the president and had been ushered into the man's office. Later, a safety-deposit box had been provided for his dusty, still-swollen saddlebags, and he had left the bank after a highly visible handshake with the president in the bank's front lobby.

So now the town—and Tarnell—knew where the fabled gold he was carrying had been stashed; and everyone in town, including Fargo, was waiting for Tarnell to make his move.

"Do you think this Tarnell will try to rob the bank?" Mattie asked.

"I don't know," Fargo replied. "I sure as hell hope so. If he does, he'll get the surprise of his life."

"I see." She smiled. "The bank is waiting for just such a move."

"What do you think?"

"But suppose he doesn't do the obvious? Suppose he waits until poor Donna gets her share and then tries to take it from her?"

"That's why I'm waiting for him. And why I'm not giving Donna any of her share until I've seen to Tarnell."

"And all the others in this territory who would like to take it from her, as well?"

Fargo sighed. The topic was beginning to bore

him. This epic promise of his to a dying man was threatening to take over his entire life.

It was midafternoon, the day after Crooked Elk had gone back for the gold. He and Mattie were sitting in plain sight on the hotel veranda, ignoring the surprised and sometimes disapproving glances of the passing townsmen and women. A slight breeze was blowing from the mountains, and as usual, Mattie was dressed with great style. The woman had a clear appreciation of how best to set off her finer points. This was the first time she had come by since the day she had first introduced herself to him and Crooked Elk, and Fargo was pleased by her visit.

"I'll be sorry to lose Donna," Mattie continued. "She's quite an asset, you can be sure of that."

Fargo nodded. He had no doubt of that. He had felt completely and deliciously wrung out after his own marathon session with her. But an experience like that could be daunting for most men. As usual, the sexual capacity of some women never failed to amaze Fargo.

Suddenly someone ran past the hotel, shouting. Fargo and Mattie both turned. As the man neared them, they made out the words. The bank was being held up!

"Tarnell!" Fargo cried.

"Just as you planned," Mattie cried, her face flushing with excitement.

"Stay here," he told her, drawing his Colt.

He ran down the steps and across the street. Townspeople and merchants were hurrying away from the bank, while a few with drawn guns were racing toward it. Pulling up across the street from the bank, Fargo joined two hardware merchants who had ducked low behind two flour barrels. Both were toting rifles, and one had a shiny new Smith & Wesson tucked into his belt. They were excited and as nervous as cats. The bank door was wide open, and there were three horses at the hitch rack, their tails switching nervously.

"How many are in there?" Fargo asked one of the merchants, a balding fellow with a long black handlebar mustache and sleeve garters.

"There's three of them. They just walked in and told everyone to throw up their hands."

The other one, a thin-faced clerk, spoke up then. "A couple of men and old widow Tompkins were in the bank. They just turned and bolted."

"Anybody hurt?"

"Nope. The outlaws were too surprised, I reckon, to stop them."

"Three amateurs, I'm thinking," said his companion, the merchant with the handlebar mustache.

His clerk added, "They're after all that gold dust stashed in there. They asked for it special, soon as they stepped in."

Fargo nodded curtly. That was all he needed to hear. Slipping swiftly across the street, he ducked down the alley that led behind the bank. Peering in through a dirt-encrusted rear window, he caught the feverish activity of the three bank clerks as they pulled open the vault door leading to the safety-deposit box. The three outlaws were approaching the vault entrance, their backs to Fargo, but Fargo recognized the scrawny figure of Doc Gurney instantly.

That meant one of the remaining two had to be Slats Tarnell. Slats must have recruited a local gunslick. The fact that Doc Gurney was a part of this raise surprised Fargo; he had misjudged the little man. The doc had considerably more sand than Fargo had given him credit for.

The rear door led off a short porch. Fargo mounted it and with one swift kick smashed the locks. As the door swung open, Fargo charged into the bank, his Colt at the ready. He found himself in a small, glassed-in area; and from the other side of the partition, he heard Doc Gurney's sudden curse.

"It's Fargo!" he croaked.

Ducking low, Fargo dived past the partitioned area, making for the protection offered by a massive desk sitting in one corner. As he ducked behind it, the three men opened fire. Their slugs glanced off the desk's hardwood top, and from under the desk Fargo fired on the closest of the three men, Doc Gurney.

Doc gasped and dropped his Colt. Two of the clerks dashed for the counter gate while the third one threw himself bodily over the counter and fled out the door. The other two bank robbers went down on one knee to return Fargo's fire. As bullets shattered the desk's paneling, Fargo caught one of them in the arm, slamming him back into a corner.

The outlaw dropped his gun and kicked it away

from him. He sat there, staring wide-eyed at Fargo, his left hand holding his shattered arm. The other one jumped up and flung himself over the counter, breaking out of the bank. From across the street came a sudden flurry of rifle fire, and it was all over.

But something was wrong. Neither of the doc's two companions had been Slats Tarnell.

Fargo got up from behind the desk and walked over to Doc Gurney. The man was sitting up with his back to the counter, and Fargo felt a curious sadness as he looked down at the stricken man. Kneeling beside him, Fargo reached out to see how badly he was hurt.

The doc pushed his hand away. "It's fatal," the doc gasped. "No need to worry about that."

"What the hell were you trying to do?" Fargo asked him. "You're no bank robber—and neither were those two, by the looks of it."

Doc Gurney blinked up at Fargo, the trace of an ironic smile on his face. "Remember what you told me? A bullet was cleaner and quicker. I sure as hell hope you were right."

Fargo got up and stared down at the man. "Where's Slats Tarnell?"

"Beats the shit out of me, Fargo."

Then the doc's eyes lost their feverish glow and his head sagged to one side as he slumped lifeless to the floor.

Fargo had been right about one thing, anyway: a bullet *was* cleaner and quicker.

11

Mattie was atop Fargo, rocking slowly.

"This is so nice," she murmured dreamily. "I could go on like this forever."

"I'd like you to be able to," Fargo responded, "but something's happening down there I can't quite control."

"Can't you hang on for just a little while longer?"

He shook his head. "No, ma'am. Get out of my way. I'm coming down the track."

As he spoke, he reached up and grabbed her hips and began slamming her down upon his erection with an enthusiasm that caused Mattie to throw her head back and laugh. She was still laughing a moment later when she collapsed forward onto Fargo's chest. He was chuckling himself as he stroked her moist hair and let himself recover his breath.

"That will have to last me a long time," Mattie said at length, lifting her head off his chest and easing her long legs off him.

Fargo said nothing. There was no sense in saying the obvious.

"How long will you be gone?"

"I don't know. Something's wrong. I can feel it in my bones. Crooked Elk should've been back here by now."

"I know. Donna mentioned it to me."

"She's anxious to get her hands on that gold, is she?"

"Do you blame her?"

"Tell me something. When she showed up that night with the Spencer rifle and asked to stay here, was she carrying anything with her?"

"You mean gold?"

"Yes."

Mattie scooted up and rested her back against the headboard. She made a careless but not too serious attempt to cover her breasts, then glanced over at Fargo. "She did have some raw ore, yes, but she didn't know what to do with it. Then a few days later she said she got someone she entertained here to assay it for her and put what it brought in the bank."

"So she's not altogether penniless."

"I should say not."

"What's she planning to do with all this money that's coming to her?"

Mattie sighed. "San Francisco is all she can talk about. She said she'd been there as a girl and

149

always dreamed of returning, this time with enough money to start her own house."

"I see."

Mattie looked at Fargo reprovingly. "It may not sound like such a lofty goal to you, Fargo. But women like us, it's all we have to look forward to in our old age."

"I suppose so."

"Come here."

He pushed himself up beside her. She took his face in her hands and pulled him gently to her, then kissed him. It was a warm, lovely kiss—unlike any she had bestowed on him before.

"What was that for?" he asked, surprisingly moved.

"For being the man you are," she said. "For keeping your promise, I guess."

"I haven't kept it yet—and that's what's bothering me."

"You will," she said. "I know you will."

The next evening, after being on the trail since sunup, Fargo found a stream in a wooded valley and built a campfire. As he was placing the coffee-pot on the flames, he glanced up to catch the last rays of the setting sun. He caught something else as well: the glint of a rifle barrel on a ridge halfway up the timbered slope. Without letting on he'd seen anything, he gathered more firewood and piled it beside the fire. Twice he went into the pines for more kindling. The third time he stayed in the timber and with his Colt out ran swiftly up the needle-clad slope until he was above the ridge.

He spotted the rifleman as he disappeared into the pines below the ridge. All Fargo saw, in the instant before he vanished, was the rifleman's hat and shoulders. Angling down onto the ridge, Fargo scrambled over the rocky outcropping, dropped to the pine needles, and moved swiftly and silently into the dark timber. He caught up with his quarry close to the bottom of the slope just as the fellow was slipping cautiously out from behind a large tree.

Fargo was a few steps from him when a pine cone crunched under his foot. The fellow started to turn. Fargo swung his Colt, its heavy barrel catching the man on the side of his head. The fellow dropped his rifle and went tumbling backward over a windfall. Fargo leapt over the downed tree and crunched down upon the man, elation building within him, certain he had finally caught up with Slats Tarnell.

But as soon as he grabbed the rifleman by the shoulder and hauled his face up to what little light filtered through the heavy pines, Fargo swore softly—in a curious mixture of frustration and sorrow. With the barrel of his Colt, he had just clubbed Donna Alvarez.

When he couldn't slap her awake, he slung her over his shoulder, picked up her rifle, and lugged her on down the slope to his campfire, where he dumped her on the ground, none too gently. What in the hell, he wondered, was she doing up on that ridge tracking him with a Spencer?

When she regained consciousness a few minutes later, he asked her.

"I was following you," she said, her hand massaging her aching head.

"With a rifle?"

"It's mine. I know how to use it."

"I know that. Were you planning on using it on me?"

"Of course not. I was just following you."

"Why?"

"I want to come with you."

"Why?"

"That gold. It is mine. You say so yourself."

"You're share of it is."

"You see? So when Mattie tell me where you go, I follow." She lifted her hand to a particularly tender spot and winced. "Why you hit me so hard?"

"I didn't know it was you."

"You cannot tell man from woman?"

"It was dark in the pines."

She looked at him for a long minute, then shrugged. "I forgive you. That coffee. I smell it from way up there. You think it ready by now?"

It was more than ready, but neither of them complained as they downed the pot's black contents. Donna told him where she'd left her horse, and Fargo went for it. When he returned, she had already finished getting his bedroll ready—for both of them, from the looks of it.

"Now," she said as she flipped the blanket aside for him, "I make you pay for hitting me. You will get little sleep this night."

Fargo looked down at her. She was as naked as a plucked chicken, but a damn sight more interesting. "Aren't you afraid of mosquitoes?"

"Hurry up," she commanded.

With a dutiful sigh, Fargo kicked off his boots.

One look at Crooked Elk's cabin and Fargo knew there was trouble. Bad trouble.

"Stay here," he told Donna.

"But why?"

"Just do as I say!"

They were on foot. As a precaution, he had decided they should dismount a couple of hundred yards lower on the slope and had tethered their mounts in a clump of alder.

"And keep down."

Donna ducked behind a boulder as Fargo moved swiftly toward the cabin, darting up the steep slope. The cabin door hung open on one leather hinge. No smoke came from the chimney, and Fargo could see no sign of Crooked Elk's horse or burro. The place had the look of death and abandonment about it, and a cold hand was closing about his heart as he drew his Colt and darted the few remaining yards to the door and burst into the cabin.

He found what he had not wanted to find.

The first thing that came to his mind was that the Apaches had followed him from the border. Only an Apache mind coupled with Apache patience could have so reduced Crooked Elk to this horror. The man hung, head down, from the cabin's main beam, his completely skinned body alive with murmuring flies. There were no fingernails left, no scalp, and only a black, crawling hole where his crotch had been. It was obvious that it had taken a very long time for Crooked Elk to die, and the thought caused Fargo to turn away and reach out to the doorjamb to brace himself.

Donna's cry came up to him from the slope below. She was asking if she could join him now.

"Stay where you are," he managed.

The last thing he wanted was for Donna to see what had been done to Crooked Elk. He dragged over a chair and, stepping up onto it, waved off the flies and used his bowie to cut down Crooked Elk's body. Grabbing his ankles, he dragged what was left of his friend over to his cot and up onto it. He used some rawhide to tie the bearskin coverlet around Crooked Elk's body.

Numb with grief and anger, Fargo left the cabin and started down the slope to get Donna. He had taken only a few steps when he heard a familiar laugh to his right. Swinging around, he saw Slats Tarnell step out from behind a clump of pine. One arm was around Donna's waist and his other hand was holding a knife to her throat. Between them yawned a gully. Tarnell stepped closer to its edge, then sheathed his knife and flung Donna to the ground. When Donna struck it, she cried out more in confusion and surprise than pain. So far, she hadn't been injured seriously, Fargo was grateful to see.

Tarnell was wearing a black stetson, Levi's, and a

leather, buttonless vest over a red cotton shirt. Slung over one shoulder were two empty saddle-bags. "Where's that gold you hid, Fargo?" he called. "Tell me or I'll mess up your pretty traveling companion."

"It was you?" Fargo said as much in astonishment as anger. "You're the one who did that to Crooked Elk?"

"That's right, Fargo," Tarnell said, a trace of pride in his voice. "I'm the one strung him up and skinned him. He sure was a tough old bastard. Wouldn't tell me nothing."

"You son of a bitch."

"Hell, Fargo. Didn't you know that?" He took out his Colt and aimed it down at Donna and fired. A geyser of dirt and stones exploded inches from her face. He cocked his weapon again, then placed his boot on her neck and ground her head into the dirt.

Fargo still had his Colt. He knew he could raise it and fire before Tarnell could get off an accurate shot at him. But at this distance there was a chance he might hit Donna.

"You watching, Fargo?" Tarnell called. "I'm going to count to three. Then I'm going to blow her pretty little nose off, unless you tell me where you got that gold hid."

"All right. I'll tell you. Leave her be."

Tarnell chuckled. "First you unbuckle your gun belt and throw it down the slope. And do it real careful like."

Fargo did as he was told.

Tarnell smiled and lowered his Colt. "That's better. Now, where's the gold? That's all I want. The gold. Then I'll leave you be—both of you."

"How do I know I can trust you?"

"You don't. Hell, maybe you can't. But that's just the chance you're going to have to take."

Fargo caught something in Slats Tarnell's eyes he had seen on only rare occasions, the red light of madness. It was the gold fever that had done it—that and his hatred of Fargo. Both had been building in him since that showdown south of Tularosa. Now the man was completely unhinged. Reasoning with him would make as much sense as trying to talk a grizzly out of a honey tree.

Abruptly, Donna lifted her head to say something to Tarnell. Before she could get a word out, he kicked her in the face so hard she must have been unconscious before her head hit the ground. So fast did it happen, she didn't even cry out.

Tarnell looked at Fargo. "All right. Let's hear it," Tarnell called. "Where's the gold hid?"

"Get away from her first, or I'll tell you nothing."

With a mean laugh, Tarnell fitted his boot in under Donna's waist and kicked her down into the gulley. She rolled slowly first, then began to tumble awkwardly down the steep slope. It was a long fall, and when Donna finally came to rest against the base of some saplings far below, Fargo couldn't be sure she was still alive.

"You dirty bastard," Fargo said.

Tarnell shrugged. "Hell. I did what you wanted. Only I let *her* get away from me. Now, tell me where that gold is or I'll use her carcass for a target. She'll look like a piece of bloody Swiss cheese when I get through with her. Now, talk."

"It's in a cave."

"How far?"

"On the slope up there," Fargo said, motioning with his head. "Behind that boulder."

Glancing up at it, Tarnell grinned. "I thought it was something like that. There was sure as hell no gold in that half-breed's cabin."

"You want me to take you to it?"

"That's what I want, boss. Get over here."

Fargo scrambled down the steep side of the gulley and up the graveled far side. He was hoping he'd get a chance to take Slats, but as soon as Fargo pulled himself up out of the gulley, Slats clubbed him on the side of the head, almost sending him back down into the gulley.

Fargo looked up groggily at Tarnell, and Tarnell grinned malevolently in return. "That was for openers," Tarnell said. "Now get up. Real slow. And keep on ahead of me."

His head throbbing, Fargo moved past the cabin and up the steep, talus-littered slope to the ridge where the great boulder rested like a huge white cauliflower blossoming out of the mountain.

"The cave's in behind there," Fargo said. "The entrance's behind some scrub pine."

Tarnell shook his head in admiration, his Colt still in his hand. "Never would have guessed there was a cave there. Looks like that boulder is pressed right into that mountain. Get at it."

"I'm telling you where the gold is. Get it yourself."

Tarnell laughed and lashed out with his Colt. Fargo ducked and tried to grab the gun from Tarnell's hand, but the man was quick enough to pull the gun back, then lash out with it, catching Fargo's forearm. As Fargo staggered under the blow, Tarnell stepped in closer and clubbed Fargo on the head, driving the Trailsman to his knees.

Fargo shook his head groggily, dimly aware of Tarnell standing over him, laughing.

"That's all right," he told Fargo. "If you want me to beat on you some more, just keep on giving me trouble."

Fargo pushed himself back up onto his feet and peered at his tormentor. He had never in his life wanted to kill a man as badly as he wanted to kill Tarnell. But he knew he had to keep his wits about him—any more fool attempts to take him would very likely give Tarnell all the excuse he needed to permanently scramble his brains. Fargo moistened his dry lips and took a careful step back.

"Good," Tarnell said. "Glad to see you acting sensible. All I want now is for you to go in there and bring out that gold—all of it. And don't try anything foolish. If you do, I promise you, I'll kill that little bitch back there. I'll string her up and skin her alive just like I skinned that half-breed friend of yours." He smiled. "And you know I'll do it, don't you, boss?"

Fargo watched Tarnell as warily as he would a mad dog that might spring at any moment.

Chuckling, Tarnell flung the saddlebags he was carrying at Fargo's feet, then sat back down on a log. "Go on now," he said, waggling his Colt. "Go in there and get that gold, boss. I'll be right here waiting."

Fargo turned and headed for the boulder. Inside the cave he found the gold where he had buried it, filled the saddlebags, and left the cave. Once he was clear of the boulder, Tarnell stood up and leveled his Colt on him.

"Throw the saddlebags over here," he said.

Fargo flung them at Tarnell. They hit heavily and stayed where they landed.

"Keep in sight while I see what we got here." Tarnell told Fargo, bending down to open the nearest saddlebag. It didn't take long for Tarnell to see that all the gold was there. Satisfied, he looked up from the saddlebags at Fargo. "Now I got all the gold that was coming to me," he said, "there's just one more item on my list."

"You got the gold," said Fargo. "Light out."

"You think I'm crazy? You'd be on my tail in no time. I'd spend the rest of my life looking over my shoulder. No, sir. I'm not silly enough to let that happen."

"You're not much, are you, Tarnell? You gave your word."

"Hell, you know my word's not worth shit." He grinned. "Turn around and get back into that cave."

Fargo hesitated. Tarnell raised his Colt and fired. The slug whined off a boulder behind Fargo. Fargo ducked. Tarnell fired again. This time the ricochet nearly took off Fargo's hat. Swiftly, Fargo pulled back behind the boulder. A moment later Tarnell came at him from another angle, firing with devilish accuracy. Fargo's only course was to duck back out of sight behind the scrub pine and brush crowding the cave's entrance. But before long, Tarnell's bullets were slashing through the flimsy branches, forcing Fargo to duck back into the cave.

A minute or so later, he heard Tarnell near the cave entrance.

"Fargo!"

Fargo said nothing.

"You're going to die in there, Fargo. Buried alive! There's no other way out. I'm going to seal you in there with the bats! Think of me while you're dying." He chuckled. "And I hope it takes a long, long time."

A moment later Fargo heard a deep, distant rumbling, followed by the unmistakable sound of earth and boulders slamming down the slope. A second later what little light filtered in through the cave entrance was abruptly shut off. The rumbling continued for a moment or two longer; and then a silence, as awesome and as complete as that of the grave, enveloped Fargo.

This time it was not his imagination. He was buried alive.

12

Fargo didn't know how long he had been clawing away at the dirt and debris that clogged the cave entrance, for there was no day and no night, no dawn or dusk, no moon or stars to mark the passage of time. It wasn't that the cave was dark. It was far worse than that. Fargo found himself trapped in a universe lacking any light whatsoever.

He pulled and tugged at the dirt furiously at first, in a desperate, almost mindless attempt to claw his way out of his tomb. But when he found his breath coming in gasps, he slowed down, realizing he must conserve the amount of oxygen he was consuming. Deeper in the cave, the bats had been chirping wildly for a while, but were silent now, uttering only a feeble cry every now and then. Like Fargo, they were growing short of oxygen. Obviously, there was no other way out of this cave.

After his first frenzied efforts at clearing the entrance, Fargo became more methodical, carefully piling the dirt and small stones and boulders he dragged back through the cave entrance to one side of the cave so as to give himself more room to work. He worked steadily until pure exhaustion forced him into short, nightmarish snatches of sleep.

At last he was able to poke his head and shoulders out through the narrow entrance. His satisfaction at this accomplishment was shortlived, however, as he came up against a cold, flat, unyielding rock face that blocked all further progress. It must have come down with the rest of the debris and was now wedged firmly in between the boulder and the mountainside, sealing Fargo into his stygian tomb.

He clawed desperately at the barrier, searching its rim, hoping for a way around it. But finally, his fingers worn raw, he pushed himself back into the cave and tried not to lose heart. Sitting back on his haunches, he brushed off his hands and went over in his mind what he had to accomplish and what tools he had with which to do it. Using his hands as shovels would do him no good against that stone barrier. He needed something else—something sharp and long that would extend his reach, for what he needed to do above all else was poke a hole above or to one side of that rock; otherwise, he would suffocate before he could claw his way past the obstruction.

He spent a considerable amount of time searching the floor of the cave for a stick of some kind and finally came up with one. Only it wasn't a stick; it was a bone about a couple of feet long. It would have to do. Once again, he pushed himself out through the narrow cave entrance and with his cheek pressed hard against the damp, dirt-encrusted surface of the rock, he began to poke the bone up and around it, searching for the edge of the rock and a chance to push a hole through to the outside.

He was just about to give up when he felt the bone break through. At once he began to move the end of it about to enlarge the hole. As the hole got bigger and loose dirt and gravel cascaded down the length of his arm, grinding into his eyes and mouth, he felt the sudden, cool rush of fresh air, carrying with it the scent of pine needles.

He almost cried out in joy; never before had anything smelled so good to him as that first, cool rush of night air. Now, at least, he wouldn't suffocate. He was still trapped, since he doubted if he could claw past this enormous block of stone. But now he had more time.

He was about to pull the bone back in when he felt someone grab it!

He yanked back on the bone, then poked it out once more. Again there was a tug on it. He pulled it down beside him and shouted, "Who is it? Who's out there?"

From just above him came Donna's faint, frightened voice. "It's me. Donna. Are you all right?"

"Yes!"

"What you want me to do?"

"Go back to Crooked Elk's cabin. Bring his shovel. Make that hole bigger."

"All right," she cried.

He heard her dimly as she scrambled down the wall of dirt enclosing him; then he took a deep breath and pushed himself back into the cave. He was going to make it, by God! He was going to make it. He and the bats were going to visit the outside world once more!

Once the hole above the boulder was larger, Fargo could communicate more easily with Donna. Though he soon found that the opening could never be made large enough for him to crawl through, it was sufficiently large to enable her to hand the shovel down to him, along with some candles and matches. He then instructed her to find a fallen limb that was at least six or seven feet long. Anything longer, he knew she wouldn't be able to poke through the cave entrance at an angle.

She found a limb and managed to push it down to the cave entrance. Fargo pulled it the rest of the way in, then thrust one end of the limb back out through the cave entrance, ramming it as far as he could in under the stone blocking his way out. Using as a fulcrum a boulder he had earlier dragged close to the entrance, he stood on the far end of the branch and felt the huge rock lift slightly. His theory proving feasible, he proceeded to roll a huge rock he had found far back in the cave toward the branch. It was a long and tedious task, testing Fargo's endurance and strength to their limits, but at last he managed to roll the rock onto the end of the branch. The branch dug into the fulcrum, then once again lifted the rock.

Holding a flickering candle in his hand, Fargo poked his head out of the cave entrance to see how far off the ground his lever had raised the rock. It was up about half a foot off the ground at the most. Reaching in under it, he felt the ground. It was pebbly and soft. He went back for the shovel and for the next two hours dug the dirt out from under the rock until he had fashioned a narrow tunnel. When at last he saw daylight on the far end, he passed the shovel back out to Donna. Swiftly, she enlarged the hole at the other end.

What he had now was a passageway under the rock. It was no wider than his body. If he had guessed right, it was large enough to allow him to crawl through all the way to the other side. If the lever continued to hold and if the opening at the other end was wide enough to allow his broad shoulders to pass through, he'd make it.

But if any of those calculations were wrong, he would die under that massive stone—crushed like a fly under a boot heel.

He went back into the cave to check the lever once more. The huge boulder was still holding it in place, but he noticed a growing crack in the branch on the cave side of the fulcrum. It was only a matter of time before the branch gave way completely under that enormous weight. And the boulder he was using for a fulcrum was settling deeper into the floor of the cave. All of which meant he didn't have a moment to lose.

"I'm coming out," he shouted.

He could just barely hear her response as he took a deep breath and pushed himself out through the cave entrance, then ducked his head under the rock and began to inch his way through the tunnel. More than once he imagined he could feel the rock settling down upon him, and there were times when he became wedged so firmly between the ground and its underside that he became almost certain the branch holding it above him had already snapped. But he kept going, measuring his progress in inches, until the sweet, cool air rushing into his laboring lungs told him he was almost there. Then he felt a fresh wind tugging at the hair on top of his head.

Then his head was out. But not his shoulders. They were caught! Desperately, he wriggled them, filled suddenly with a mindless, unreasoning panic. What if now, after all this, the rock settled down on him, breaking his back and trapping him irrevocably.

But by then Donna had her hands about his shoulders and was pulling him free. Like a cork popping from a bottle, he scrambled out and jumped to his feet. It was the morning of a bright, lovely day. He could feel the wind on his cheeks and everywhere he looked he saw sights he'd almost given up hope of ever seeing again. Trees. Fleecy clouds in a blue sky. Donna.

He grabbed her about the waist and flung her around in a circle. Then he began to laugh. Donna was as excited as he was, laughing and crying at the same time.

*   *   *

They buried Crooked Elk before they set out after Slats Tarnell later that same afternoon. Then Fargo bade Donna wait for him while he rode back up to the cave entrance. He wanted to look once more on the site of what could have been his tomb.

As he pulled up before the huge boulder, he found it difficult to believe that his entombment had lasted only a day and a half. It had seemed like a century. Looking the site over more calmly now, he shook his head in wonderment when he saw how incredibly lucky he'd been. Had he dug that tunnel in any other direction, he'd have been stopped cold. A few degrees to the left, he would have struck the huge boulder that had originally served to hide the cave entrance. Had he dug only a few degrees farther to the right, he'd have been burrowing futilely into the base of the mountain.

He shuddered at the thought. The memory of his cold, dark tomb would fuel many a nightmare to come. He had Slats Tarnell to thank for that.

And for the death of Crooked Elk as well.

Fargo turned his pinto and started back down the slope to rejoin Donna. She had explained to him how she had scrambled back up onto her feet and followed Tarnell and him up the mountain. She'd caught up to them just as Tarnell forced Fargo back into the cave, then watched helplessly as Tarnell nudged the huge rock down the slope, initiating the avalanche that buried the cave entrance.

Tarnell never returned to the gully and must have assumed either that Donna was dead or that she posed no threat to him. For Tarnell just rode off.

Weaponless, Donna was unable to stop him, but she marked well the direction he took before she began her frantic effort to dig Fargo out. She had been about to give up when that bone poked through.

"Ready?" Donna asked. The side of her face was raw from the punishment she'd taken from the slope and Tarnell. A hardness in her face reminded Fargo that this was the same woman who had left a man to die with a knife in his back while he slowly twisted on the end of a rope deep in a mine shaft.

"I'm ready," Fargo told her.

"Let us go, then. That son of a bitch, he has my gold."

"Mine, too," Fargo reminded her.

"Of course," she said, turning her horse.

As they rode after Tarnell, Fargo found himself studying Donna closely. The first thing she had said to him, once the first flush of excitement at his remarkable deliverance had passed, was that now, with him free, she would regain her gold from Tarnell.

It was the gold then, more than any loyalty or feeling for him, that had kept her by the cave entrance, digging away at that pile of earth and rubble. She needed his gun and his tracking ability if she were ever to see that gold Walt Tennyson had left her.

*   *   *

Since there was a full moon, they were able to keep on Tarnell's trail throughout the night. And a day later, after stopping only for catnaps, they found themselves moving into higher country. Twice since morning Fargo dismounted to study Tarnell's tracks, each time marking the furious pace he was setting. He had no reason to keep up such a pace; but then, Fargo recalled, Tarnell was never one to care too deeply for his mounts anyway. He'd soon ride this horse into the ground, Fargo figured, especially considering the load of gold he was carrying.

About noon they passed through a ravine and found themselves moving across a sunlit parkland. The ground was baked hard and the shallow grass was burned by the sun, making Tarnell's tracks a bit harder to follow; but thanks to the gold it was carrying, his horse was making tracks deep enough, even on this terrain, for Fargo to follow.

A stream appeared off to their left, tumbling swiftly through a cleft in a patch of caprock. Its course was marked by a green line of cottonwood and aspen. Fargo swung his pinto in that direction.

"We'd better rest and water the horses," Fargo told Donna. "And rest ourselves some, too."

Grudgingly Donna followed his lead.

As the two dismounted under a cottonwood, Fargo glanced at Donna. "Did you notice Tarnell's tracks?"

Donna frowned. "What you mean?"

"They went right on past this stream. Tarnell

sure is doing his best to run that horse of his into the ground."

She shrugged. "I not notice such things."

They watered their horses, then set them loose to graze for a while. Fargo lay back full length on some warm caprock, his arms folded under his head, and watched the tiny puffs of cloud drift across the sky. The sight was still a wonder to him after what he had been through. Never again, he told himself, would he take the sun and the sky for granted.

After a while he glanced over at Donna. She was sitting with her back to a tree, watching him. She seemed puzzled.

"What's wrong, Donna?"

"You."

"What do you mean?"

"You will let him get away. You lay back on the ground and look up at the sky like little boy on holiday with nothing else to do."

"We're keeping our horses healthy by resting them. We won't catch Tarnell on foot."

Donna said nothing, and again Fargo studied her. Sh'd been upset at finding that Tarnell had taken her Spencer with him when he rode off. That rifle seemed to matter a great deal to her. He guessed he could understand that. He was glad he still had his Colt and the Sharps. Both weapons had been with him a long time.

He leaned back and closed his eyes, feeling the wind playing with his hair as it brushed over him. Above him, the leaves moved in the wind, their sound pleasing to him. He closed his eyes and almost slept.

They continued on through the night, again sleeping only in quick snatches. Late the next day, they caught sight of a rider cresting the ridge ahead of them. He was about a mile away. As horse and rider stood out sharply for a moment, the rider turned in his saddle. Sunlight glinted on metal. Then he was gone.

"Do you think he sees us?" Donna asked.

"He saw us, all right."

"That mean he will wait for us up ahead, yes?"

"That's what it means, all right. You want to turn back?"

"That is not why I ask, Fargo. You know that."

Fargo shrugged. "Just want to make sure you know what you're getting into."

The next morning they passed through a long ravine, and Fargo dismounted to study Tarnell's tracks. He saw what he'd been waiting for: Tarnell's horse was close to foundering. Swinging up into his saddle, he peered at the trail ahead of them. It was winding and treacherous, with any number of vantage points from which to fire down upon pursuers.

Fargo looked at Donna. "I'll go ahead. You stay about fifty yards behind. No sense in giving Tarnell a clear shot at both of us."

Startled, Donna looked quickly about. "Do you think he's close by?"

"I'm not sure. Just being careful."

They rode on for close to an hour before Fargo spotted the dead horse on the trail ahead. Barely visible at first, it reminded Fargo of a woman's oversized purse gleaming in the sun. Glancing up, he saw two buzzards hanging in the sky high above the cliffs still looming over the trail.

Donna overtook him as they approached the dead animal.

"Keep an eye out," he told her.

They were almost to the dead horse when a rifle cracked above them, its shattering roar echoing through the canyon. As the bullet slammed off a rock beside him, Fargo grabbed his Sharps and hurled himself from his saddle, making for a huge boulder beside the trail. Donna was right behind him.

"He's on that ridge up there," Fargo told Donna.

He pointed and Donna nodded.

Handing Donna the Sharps and a handful of linen cartridges, he said, "Do you know how to use this?"

"My grandfather, he have one. I shoot it many times at the Apaches."

"Good. Cover me while I make for that trail beside that rock face over there."

She nodded and loaded up. He watched her for a second. She hadn't lied; the woman definitely knew how to handle the rifle. In a moment she was sending shot after shot at the ridge, and he could see the tiny explosions where the slugs were biting into the rock face. Satisfied, Fargo took out his Colt and raced out from behind the boulder. Digging

172

hard, he scrambled up the steep embankment, heading for the clump of scrub pine at its crest. He was halfway up the slope when Tarnell opened up on him. Tarnell was a good shot, Fargo had to admit, as Tarnell's rapid fire from his stolen Spencer sent geysers of sand and stone into the air all about him.

But Fargo reached the pines unscathed. Flattening himself behind a boulder, he looked back to see if he could spot Donna. He didn't have to look far. She was right behind him.

"He's still up there," Fargo told her as she dashed into the pines and pulled up beside him. Then he pointed to a game trail that led out of the timber and up the slope at a gentler angle. "I figure that will take you up past him. I'll go this way. The first one with a clear shot at him can take him. That suit you?"

"Yes," Donna said, her eyes gleaming.

Fargo waited until she had vanished up the game trail, then took off his boots and socks. Dropping both spurs and socks into his boots, he cached them behind a rock, then started up the almost sheer rock face. He headed for the beetling crown of rimrock behind which he was certain Tarnell was crouched.

His bare feet gave him excellent purchase on the rocks, and in a short time he reached the rocky overhang and pulled himself over it. Less than ten feet below him Tarnell was crouched behind a boulder, four bulging saddlebags on the ground behind him. He was aiming carefully at someone on the slope below, which meant he must have caught sight of Donna.

Leveling his Colt on Tarnell, Fargo cried, "Freeze, you son of a bitch!"

Instead, Tarnell swung around and fired at Fargo. Levering the Spencer swiftly, his rapid fire sent rounds buzzing past Fargo's head like angry wasps. Fargo got one shot off, then felt a slug tear the revolver from his hand. As it went skittering off, Donna appeared behind Tarnell. He saw her lift the Sharps and fire, but the slug somehow missed Tarnell.

Swinging around to face Donna, Tarnell ratcheted a fresh slug into his firing chamber. Too stunned by her miss to reload, Donna was caught in full view, a helpless target, transfixed with fear. Fargo unsheathed his bowie and hurled himself down the small slope with the speed of a plunging hawk. As Tarnell flung his rifle up to shoot Donna, Fargo plunged his bowie deep into the man's back.

Crying out in shock and pain, Tarnell staggered forward, the rifle in his hand blasting its charge into the ground. But as soon as Tarnell hit the ground, he caught himself and rolled over, a big Colt appearing in his right hand. It spat flame, and Fargo felt the round nick his sleeve. Reaching down before Tarnell could thumb-cock the Colt, Fargo yanked the weapon from his hand and flung it into the gorge. Then he hauled Tarnell to his feet, reached around, and none too gently pulled the bowie out of his back. Tarnell gasped, his face turning to paste from the pain. Fargo raised the knife a second time.

"Don't," he pleaded. "Don't kill me. Please! The gold. It's behind you. Take it."

"I will anyway," Fargo told him.

"Kill him," Donna cried, moving up beside Fargo.

"Is that what you want?" he asked Donna.

"Yes," she hissed.

Fargo drove his bowie deep into the man's chest. Tarnell cried out once; then his head sagged forward. Fargo removed his knife and ducked aside to escape the sudden red freshet that exploded from the man's chest. Then he sheathed the knife and with one tremendous heave lifted Tarnell over his head and flung him off the ledge. As Tarnell fell, his body bounced off two rocky outcroppings, then vanished into a pile of boulders beside the trail far below.

Fargo turned to Donna. Her face was stone white, her eyes averted. "I did not think you do it," she whispered. "Not like that."

"However you kill a man, it's never pretty."

"I did not think you do such a thing for me."

"It wasn't for you."

The tone of his voice alerted her. She looked full into his face then. "What is it you mean? He stole my gold, so you kill him."

"I killed him for what he did to Crooked Elk."

"That funny-looking half-breed?"

"Don't call him that again, Donna," Fargo said, his voice heavy with sudden menace. "I warn you."

She looked at him in surprise. "Why, Fargo! What is the matter with you? I think maybe we share this gold. How would you like to go to San Francisco with me?"

"And what would we do there?"

"Why, can you not imagine the fine big house we could run there?"

"Mattie told me about your plans. That's what you want the gold for, is it? To open up a cathouse."

"Of course! Have you ever seen San Francisco? It is the most beautiful place."

"And with lots of free-spending sailors."

She smiled slyly. "Aren't those the best kind?"

"I suppose they are," Fargo said, walking over to the saddlebags.

She followed him eagerly. "Is it all there?"

"You mean your share?"

"You know what I mean," she said eagerly. "Is it?"

"Reckon it is," Fargo said, taking out the leather pouches. He counted them out. Ten pouches for him and ten for Donna, Walt Tennyson's share. Then there was also what remained of Tarnell's gold.

"Here," he said, "hold out your arms. Here's your share of the gold, what Walt Tennyson wanted you to have."

Eagerly, she held out her hands and he carefully piled the leather pouches of gold dust into her arms. "Oh, it's so heavy," she cried delightedly.

"As heavy as a man's soul," Fargo remarked. "That's what it took to get this gold to you."

"I'm so grateful." Her greed caused her eyes to glow and put a flush in her cheeks.

"Here," he said, "dump them back in here."

"All right," she said, reluctantly dropping them back into the saddlebag.

Fargo tossed the rest of the pouches into the saddlebags also, then lugged the bags over to the edge of the ridge. With Donna looking on in bewilderment, Fargo emptied the saddlebags out again, this time onto a flat stone. Moving then with a calm deliberateness that caught Donna entirely by surprise, he untied the drawstrings and proceeded to pour out the golddust.

Screaming in sudden dismay, Donna rushed at Fargo to stop him. With a clenched right fist, he caught her flush on the chin, nearly knocking her out. As she sat down heavily on the ground and watched him with shrill dismay, he finished emptying the gold pouches—each and every one of them—into the gorge below.

13

That night Donna tried to kill him with the Spencer. After he wrested the rifle from her hands, he tied her wrists behind her and strapped her to the trunk of a tree. When she finally stopped cursing him and fell into an exhausted sleep, Fargo himself was able to get some much-needed rest.

The next morning, as they rode back to Twin Butte, Fargo decided to do some explaining, and he started by asking her if Tarnell was the man who had taken care of the raw ore she brought with her to Twin Butte, the one who had gotten it assayed for her and then banked.

"Yes," she snapped, glancing malevolently at him. "He was."

"And you told him that Crooked Elk and I did not have the gold with us. That it was hidden near Crooked Elk's cabin."

"Yes, but—"

"That was enough, Donna," Fargo interrupted. "That was all you had to do to ensure Crooked Elk's death. I guess I've known since I looked up and saw Crooked Elk's body that you had to be the one who told Tarnell. Everyone else in town—even Doc Gurney—thought your gold was in the bank. The only one who knew Crooked Elk was going after it was you. And may God forgive me, I was the one told you."

"But . . . but I didn't know Tarnell was going to kill Crooked Elk."

"You knew. And you didn't care. It was your greed that killed Crooked Elk, Donna. It wasn't just your gold you wanted, it was mine too. Did Tarnell promise you he'd share his gold with you, also?"

"Yes."

"And look how he treated you when you finally showed up."

"You cannot prove any of this."

"No, but I'm satisfied it's the truth."

"I think maybe I hate you," she said.

"I'd feel pretty damn bad, Donna, if someone with your credentials didn't."

She pulled up angrily. "I will not go back with you to Twin Butte. I will return to Tularosa."

"Don't you have some money waiting for you in the Twin Butte bank?"

"No," she told him smugly. She patted her saddlebags. "I have the money here—and I'll thank you for my rifle now."

He pulled her Spencer from his saddle scabbard,

broke it in half over his knee, and handed the pieces to her. As she threw the broken rifle to the ground, she cursed him in fluent Spanish, then hauled her horse around.

"Donna!"

She looked back at him, her face frozen with fury.

"You saved my life when I was in that cave. I saved yours back there on the mountain. We're even. But don't cross my trail again."

She flung her head around and rode off, her back stiff with anger. He watched her go, and sighed. He was sure as hell sorry it had turned out this way. He was a romantic, as Mattie insisted, and he'd thought from the beginning that if he kept his vow to Walt Tennyson, it would all turn out the way it should, with plenty of gratitude and kisses—and a fresh start for Donna Alvarez.

Well, he told himself as he nudged his Ovaro west toward Twin Butte, he'd made a vow and stuck to it. For a while there, anyway, Donna Alvarez had held in her arms Walt Tennyson's share. That much of the vow he had kept; maybe in the end, that was all that mattered.

And in a couple of days, he would see if Mattie didn't agree with him.

LOOKING FORWARD!
The following is the opening section
from the next novel in the exciting
Trailsman series from Signet:

The Trailsman #51
SIOUX CAPTIVE

1860, the wild land of Western Montana,
in the shadow of the Sapphire Mountains . . .

"This was a nice morning until you came along,
honey," the big man with the lake-blue eyes muttered.

"Abigail, I told you. Abigail Snow," the young
woman snapped.

"A white-winged dove sang real pretty. This little
stream made a nice, tinkly sound, and the pocket
gophers set up a soft chatter," the big man went on.
"Since you showed up, I've heard nothing but your
cackling."

"That's just too damn bad," the young woman
threw back, her lips tight. The big man surveyed
her again as he bent down to the stream to fill his
canteen. She had light-brown hair, cut short and

full of curls, direct brown eyes, a thin nose, and a long, narrow figure with modest breasts that pushed upward against a light-blue cotton blouse. She'd be really pretty if she stopped holding her face so prim and severe, he decided. "Hasn't the thought of being a good Samaritan ever crossed your mind, Mr. Fargo?" she snapped.

"Yes, ma'am, and it usually crosses right on out," Skye Fargo answered as he finished filling the canteen.

"I've offered you good money," she said.

"And I answered you on that," he returned. He watched her mouth thin as he rose to his feet and tightened the lid on the canteen.

"Dammit, a Sioux runs off with a helpless little boy. Doesn't that reach you at all? Don't you feel anything?" she accused.

"I feel sorry," he said.

"Is that all? Have you no conscience?"

"I've a conscience. I let common sense keep it down," he answered.

"Meaning what?" She glared.

"Meaning that that Sioux could be anywhere by now and the boy dead. It happened a week ago, you say," Fargo told her.

"But maybe he's still alive. We have to try to find him," the young woman insisted.

"It's plain he's not your boy." Fargo frowned at her.

"He's my sister's boy," Abigail said.

He shrugged. "Makes no matter. I told you, I've got a job to do," he said.

"I knew that before you told me," she said, and he felt his one thick black eyebrow lift. "You're going to Ironwood to pick up a wagon train. That's why I chased after you. My sister lives just outside town."

"Who told you all this, honey?" Fargo asked.

"Ben Hibbs," she said, and Fargo half-smiled. Ben was a post rider who knew pretty much what everyone was up to in his territory. He let his gaze move out from the little glen by the stream. Low hills surrounded it on three sides, a perfect spot to rest and relax. Or it had been, he grunted as Abigail's voice cut into his thoughts, an edge of accusation in it.

"You could combine both jobs," she pushed at him.

He tossed her a glance of pained tolerance. "Can't break trail for a wagon train and go chasing some crazy Sioux," Fargo said.

"You could give it a try," she said, and suddenly a note of desperate pleading had come into her voice.

He eyed her narrow, high-busted figure, and saw her try to keep the pleading out of her face as she continued to regard him accusingly.

"I'd do right by no one," Fargo answered, and a tiny frown touched his brow. "Why'd you come looking for me? Why not the boy's mother?" he asked.

"There are reasons. They don't concern you unless you're taking the job," she said stiffly.

"Fair enough," he agreed. "Sorry, go find yourself another tracker."

"I can't. It'd take too long," she snapped angrily. "Besides, I'm told you're the very best."

"And I told you I'm spoken for. I've given my word. I won't go back on it," he said as he hung the canteen on the saddle and stroked the magnificent black-and-white Ovaro.

"Your word to a bunch of farmers and misfits looking for a new start. They can wait," she sniffed disdainfully.

"You see things as they suit you to see them." He smiled. "But then that's what most folks do. But I made an agreement. I'll stand by it."

Anger flared in the direct, brown eyes and her pretty face grew hard. "Or maybe it's just a lot safer to lead a wagon train than to track down a Sioux," she speared waspishly.

She was calling him a coward, but he laughed as he refused to take the bait. "Might be," he agreed pleasantly.

"Damn you," she swore as she spun on her heel and strode back to her horse.

He watched her halt alongside the animal and rest her forehead against the saddle skirt for a moment. When she raised her head, she turned again and walked back to where Fargo waited beside the little stream. Her face now held resignation in it, and there was a sad beauty to her. "Maybe you'll think about it some more," she said. "I'm asking that of you."

"Fair enough," he said, and she thrust a piece of paper at him.

"That's where you can reach me in Ironwood in case you change your mind," she said.

Under the demanding anger, her concern for the boy was plainly very real, he realized. He felt sorry for her, but he wouldn't go back on his word. But he'd no wish to pull all hope out from under her, and he took the piece of paper and pushed it into his pocket. He returned to his horse with her, halted there as she started to move on. He espied one of the saddle strings had come loose, bent down to fix it when the shot exploded in the little glen. He felt the bullet graze the side of his head, and he let himself pitch forward onto the ground as the horse instinctively skittered away. Abigail's scream cut through the air as he lay facedown and motionless.

The shot had come from the low rise to the north, the gunman undoubtedly still in position to fire again. It was time to play possum or he'd draw another shot that wouldn't miss. He lay still and listened to the sound of a horse galloping closer, skidding to a halt, and the rider slide from the saddle.

"Get the hell back, sister," he heard the man's voice rasp.

Fargo's eyes seemed to be closed but tiny, unnoticeable slits let him have a narrow, truncated view of nearby objects. He heard the footsteps walk toward him, halt. He felt the toe of the man's boot wedge itself under his chest. The man pushed and lifted with his foot, and Fargo let himself be turned limply onto his back. Through his slitted eyelids he glimpsed the end of the man's rifle barrel. He'd have but one chance, he knew as the man's legs came into his view, but he continued to play dead.

He felt the man kick him in the side and he let his body shake lifelessly. The man was plainly uncertain, and Fargo saw the rifle barrel lower as the man bent over him for a closer check. Fargo tensed muscles, held still a fraction longer, and suddenly flung his right arm stiffly outward to slam into the man's ankles with the force of a two-by-four.

"Shit," the man cursed as he toppled forward, the rifle firing as his finger tightened on the trigger. Fargo felt the shot plow into the ground alongside him, but he was rolling now as the gunman pitched forward half over him. He got one knee up and sank it into the man's ribs as the bushwhacker fell across him. He heard the man grunt in pain. Fargo continued to roll, halted his momentum, came up on one knee to see the man, the rifle still in his hands, fire from half on his side.

Fargo flung himself sideways onto the ground as

the rifle blast passed over his head, rolled again, and dived into a thicket of heavy underbrush. He yanked the big Colt from its holster as the bush-whacker fired again. Fargo heard the bullet snapping off twigs and leaves as it passed through. But he had the Colt aimed as the man realized he was out in the open and tried to scramble for the brush behind him.

Fargo fired and the man cried out in pain as he clutched at his leg and fell. But he still clung to his rifle, and Fargo saw him try to pull the gun around to fire. The Colt barked again and the rifle flew into the air as the man cursed and clutched at his right hand. He started to scramble for the bushes again when Fargo's shot threw up a little geyser of soil directly in front of his face. The man froze in place, one bleeding hand still dug into the ground.

Fargo's quick glance saw that Abigail had backed to one side, her eyes round and wide with fright. He returned his gaze to the man still in place on the ground.

"You stay right there, you bushwhacking son of a bitch," Fargo said. "I want some answers out of you."

"Go to hell," the man snapped as he half-turned onto his back.

Fargo let the click of the hammer being drawn back on the Colt sound through the little glen. "Talk or I'm going to shoot you apart piece by piece," he growled.

"Screw you, mister," the man returned.

Fargo let the Colt fire, and a toe of the man's left foot blew away. The man screamed in pain and drew his leg up as he stared down at his bloodied foot.

"Talk," Fargo growled from the brush.

"Goddamn bastard," the man shouted back, pain in his voice.

Fargo fired again and this time the man's right kneecap erupted in a shower of blood and bone chips. The man cried out as he rolled onto his side in pain. "Goddamn," he said breathlessly, and clutched at his leg.

"Piece by piece," Fargo repeated from the thicket.

"You son of a bitch," the man cursed.

Fargo fired again and this time the man's right elbow disintegrated, and he half-flew onto his other side as his wild scream of pain echoed. "Piece by piece," Fargo said.

"All right, shit . . . all right," the man shouted in pain and terror. "I'll talk, I'll talk."

Fargo half-rose in the thicket, his gun still aimed at the man. Abigail had remained in place, and she stared at the man on the ground with a frown. "I'm waiting," Fargo said. "And I'm out of patience."

Fargo saw the man curled up in pain start to lick his lips as the rifle shot exploded. Fargo dropped down, an instant, automatic reaction. But even as he did so, he saw the figure on the ground grab at his chest as the shot slammed into him. Fargo's eyes flashed to the nearest hilltop in time to see the horse's gray rump disappear down the other side of the rise.

"Goddamn," he swore as he stood up and stepped out of the thicket. The man on the ground was rapidly becoming a huge, lifeless red stain that spread from his shattered chest. Fargo shot a glance at Abigail. "You all right?" he asked, and she nodded, shock still in her face.

His eyes returned to the low rise, and he cursed softly. By the time he mounted the Ovaro, the bushwhacker would be at the bottom of the rise and racing hard into thick tree cover. He brought his gaze back to the crumpled object that lay at his feet, and grimaced. "Shit," he muttered as he stared down at the lifeless form, and Abigail slowly moved to stand behind him.

"What'd you expect he'd tell you?" Abigail asked. "It's plain they were a pair of saddle bums who thought they'd found an easy dollar."

"Were they?" Fargo said as he turned his lake-blue eyes on her.

"Of course." Abigail frowned back.

"Try again," Fargo answered.

Her frown deepened. "What are you saying?" she asked.

"I'm saying they were no bushwhackers out for an easy dollar. They were here to make sure you didn't hire me," he told her, and watched her lovely lips fall open.

"That's impossible. It's crazy," Abigail protested.

"Why'd they try to nail only me?" Fargo pushed at her.

"I guess they figured with you out of the way they could have their way with me," she returned.

"Good enough except it doesn't fit these two. They were watching from the low rise but didn't make a move until they saw you give me that piece of paper," he said.

"Meaning what?" Abigail asked.

"From where they were it looked as though you'd given me the money to seal the deal, and I'd taken it. That's when the first one fired," Fargo said. Abigail's frown held as her brown eyes grew darker. "When the attack backfired, an ordinary bushwhacker would have taken off. But the second one waited until he heard the other one say he'd talk. He made sure he didn't and then hightailed it."

Abigail's face held protest and shock as his words mingled with disbelief. "Why?" she murmured. "Why would anyone want to stop me from trying to save a little boy's life?"

Fargo shrugged, his handsome, intense face made of chiseled stone. "I thought maybe you'd tell me." he said.

Exciting Westerns by Jon Sharpe

(0451)

*Prices slightly higher in Canada

**Buy them at your local
bookstore or use coupon
on next page for ordering.**

Exciting Westerns by Jon Sharpe